KINGS OF CHAOS

Crossfire

KENTUCKY

Charles Kelley

CROSSFIRE

Book 2 in the Kings of Chaos Motorcycle Club series

By Charles Kelley

For my boys Conner & Crew; I'll always have your back.

ACKNOWLEDGMENTS

To everyone who read Crossroads and encouraged me to keep going, this is your fault. See what you started? But seriously, thank you. Your support has been overwhelming and extremely appreciated. This is for all of you, and I hope you enjoy it!

A big-time thanks also goes out to Andrew Miller for your invaluable feedback during the editing process of this story. This book would be much less coherent without your uncanny ability to understand what I'm trying to say and offer suggestions on how to adapt my thoughts so they actually make sense!

I also need to recognize Adam K. Moore and Christian Scully for being crucial sounding boards. Your willingness to listen to my incessant driveling about ideas and helping me work through writer's block is appreciated beyond measure.

Chapter 1

BEEP, BEEP.

BEEP, BEEP.

I awake to the sound of a heart monitor counting out my pulse. My throat is sore as shit from being intubated. I slowly open my eyes and am flooded with bright lights. Everything is a blur for what seems like minutes, but in reality might've been twenty seconds. Once my eyes come into focus, I glance around the room. I can't move my head because of the neck brace I'm tethered to, but I still manage to spot Kayla sitting in a chair by the window. Her long brown hair absorbs the light around her, helping my eyes to focus on her beauty. She must've sensed my gaze, turning from the window she flashes me a huge smile and steps over to my bedside, leaning down and kissing me on the cheek. Without speaking, she leaves the room for a split second and comes back in with her brother Scott in tow, who's sporting his Kings of Chaos Motorcycle Club colors. Now I don't know how long I've been out, but I don't see any possible way the club could have survived the subsequent sting that I coordinated. He approaches the bed, and I notice the patch on his chest - Prez. What the hell?

He must've read my mind as he started talking. "I'm picking up the pieces," he acknowledges. "But this time, I'm doing it my way. The right way." He turns his back to me so I can see the colors. Noticeably absent is the diamond-shaped 1%er patch, signifying that the club is on a more legitimate path. "You get better quick, because I'm gonna need some help with this. What good is a Prez without a righteous VP?" he grins before leaving the room.

Good for you, kid. "You know, you're gonna need more than that scooter if you wanna keep wearing that "P" patch," I croak, unsure if my voice even makes it to his ears.

"Your smartass never misses a beat, does it?" Kayla asks, chiding me for already giving her brother shit within two minutes of waking up. She looks into my eyes, and I see nothing but appreciation and adoration. What a difference a week makes. Before she and I can connect any further, in walks the doctor. Impeccable timing, ya jerk.

"Mr. McGee, glad to see you're awake. How are you feeling?"

"Come on, doc. Look at me. You know I'm not feeling anything, and if I *was* feeling something then it wouldn't be anything good."

"Fair point. I'm sure you have a lot of questions, so let me see if I can fill in some of the blanks for you," he offers. "When you first arrived to the ER following your accident, you were on the brink of death. You are very fortunate to be with us today given the spill you and your motorcycle took. Luckily, your body went limp when you went airborne. I assume you were already unconscious, and that is what saved your life. Being loose like a ragdoll kept your injuries from being worse…not that they're good by any means. We've had you sedated for about three weeks now to make the ventilator more tolerable while your lung healed."

Three weeks?!

"You broke both legs, your pelvis, right arm and wrist. Your right shoulder was also dislocated. Eight ribs were cracked, puncturing your right lung. You fractured three vertebrae and had severe swelling in your brain, causing a massive concussion. So if you notice an aversion to bright lights that would be why."

"Well damn, doc. Is that all?" I say, sarcastically, suddenly aware of the pain caused by breathing. I see both of my legs are still in plaster casts, and held in a raised position by an intricate pulley system. My right arm is in a sling and also casted from the elbow to my thumb. I notice for the first time that the overhead lights in my room are off. I probably should've noticed that right off the bat, what with the aforementioned neck brace limiting my field of vision to directly straight up and whatnot.

"Obviously, we have you on some pretty serious pain meds to make your consciousness tolerable. You can plan on being here awhile longer so we can monitor your recovery. Seems like you are a pretty important person to someone who can pull strings, and they want to make sure you are well taken care of."

Thank goodness for the DEA and my government benefits.

Let me catch you up real quick. My name's Will McGee. You may remember me from such stories as my last one. My childhood was ruined by a bunch of degenerate bikers, so I grew up and came back to ruin their adulthood. Unfortunately, since *I'm* the one in the hospital, it seems that didn't work out as planned.

I was born and raised in the tiny town of Rough River Falls, Kentucky, by a father who didn't really have much of an interest in being a father. He lived his life on the back of a 1948 Harley-Davidson panhead, riding alongside a bunch of other irresponsible assholes under the guise of a motorcycle club calling themselves the Kings of Chaos. Raising me was an afterthought. When I finally turned 18, I ran away to the United States Air Force and became a cop. That's where I really found myself and discovered who I was and who I was meant to be. It was also during this time that my dad's bad habits finally caught up to him and put him out of his misery.

After six years serving this great country, I separated from the USAF and was recruited to join the Drug Enforcement Agency. It turned out, just prior to my separation from the Air Force, the Kings of Chaos were directly responsible for a cocaine overdose of a Kentucky State Representative's son, Brad Olsen. Given my connections, the DEA found my personal history and timing invaluable. My recruitment to the Agency was based solely on my ability to infiltrate the Kings and bring them down from the inside…and boy, let me tell you, did shit ever go down!

For better or worse, depending on who you are and how you want to look at it, I got tangled up with a couple locals upon my return to Rough River Falls. I had grown up with Kayla, but it wasn't until my return to the area before I finally recognized her beauty inside and out. I was familiar with her growing up of course, with it being such a small town, but I was always too busy wallowing in self-pity to pay attention to anybody that wasn't in my immediate personal space. By spending more time with her, I naturally spent more time with her younger brother, Scott, by default. I learned of their heart-wrenching family history, with their parents being killed in a car accident while they were still teenagers, and I learned of Scott's downward spiral and lowly stature in the town. Because nothing in life can ever be simple and straightforward, I also learned about his association with the Kings that followed the accident. Scott is the only member of the club that I give a shit about, and he's the only one that managed to avoid incarceration following my investigation and bust. Everybody still with me? Good. Moving on.

"So how long am I gonna be laid up in here, doc?" Enough chit chat. Healed up or not, all I could think is, it's time to get back to business.

"Well, obviously you're going to have a long and likely slow recovery with a lot of painful physical therapy," he advised. "And that's just to get out of here. Once you finally get discharged, you'll have to go to a rehab facility to continue the process for probably another month or so."

I don't like the sound of that at all.

"I'm no mechanic, but I have a feeling your bike has a worse prognosis."

"I'll worry about the bike, doc. You just worry about getting me ready to walk out of here."

Chapter 2

Two more weeks pass until I'm finally cleared for discharge from Grayson County Medical Center. I endured countless physical therapy sessions during my time here. It was the only way to regain some strength, stability, and range of motion. And as the doctor informed me from the outset, that was simply so I could be transferred to a rehabilitation hospital. Once there I'll focus more on fine motor function so I can resume as close to normal of a life that I had before the accident...which isn't saying much.

For the first time in over a month, I'm finally wearing my own clothes. I'm still lying in a hospital bed, which sucks, but at least my ass isn't hanging out of the back of a flimsy, single-ply, multi-purpose gown; my junk hooked up to a catheter and all that mess. I'm waiting for the doc to come in and get my discharge process in gear when I'm surprised by a vaguely familiar face.

"Will, how are you?" my DEA handler asks. I've seen several agents during my stay in the hospital, mostly assigned as a precautionary security measure, just in case the Kings still have connections and try to send somebody to shut me up – for good. This is the first time to see this face since I was involved in the shootout leading up to my accident.

"Been better. What have you been up to? Haven't seen you since my final showdown with the club."

"I've been pretty busy cleaning up your mess, as I'm sure you can imagine," he said, more than a little irritation in his tone. "I realized you still haven't had a formal debriefing following the debacle of your investigation."

Did he say "debacle?!" I happen to think it was a pretty effective and thorough job given the circumstances and my limited resources.

He continues. "The District Attorney was able to ring up most of the Kings under the RICO Act, which will be more challenging to argue and prove, but will tack on a much lengthier sentence if successful. You did provide a lot of evidence to strengthen their case, and your testimony should be the nail in the club's collective coffin."

Jackpot. Debacle my ass. Mission: accomplished.

"So, Will, you know we're going to have to pull you out of here, don't you?"

"Good. I've been waiting for the doc to come in and sign my release papers."

"Not what I meant, Will. The Agency is going to have to relocate you. For your safety and the case's."

I already knew what he was getting at. "Yeah, about that," I begin. "Listen, this is where I need to be. When I left here for the Air Force, San Antonio couldn't be far enough away from this shit-hole. Then I faced the realization of being shipped off to who-knows-where, and I didn't care much for that idea so I separated from the Air Force and came back home. This place had nothing to offer me when I was growing up, but when I came back I learned that sometimes things change. There are people here I care about and want to be here for. As far as my safety is concerned, leave that to me. I'm a big boy and have been trained by our government to be the best I can be. Don't forget how I handled myself with an entire group of outlaw bikers, who are all locked up now, by the way. Furthermore, regarding the case, y'all have my written reports, so in the event that maybe something *does* happen to me, then at least there's a paper trail."

"Regardless, Will, there's no reason for the Agency to keep you here. It's not like we're looking to create a regional office in Rough River Falls, Kentucky. Come on, let's be serious."

"Right, I get that. Try to keep up with me here. I'm not going anywhere. I'm aware the Agency has nothing for me to do here anymore, so I would venture to say that my time with the DEA has run its course. Consider this my notice of resignation. I mean, you guys are gonna have to foot these medical bills though. I didn't knock out this investigation for nothing."

"Well, I'll relay this bit of information up the chain of command then, I guess," he stammered, obviously taken aback by my statement. "All sarcasm aside, I hate to see you go, Will. You're a train wreck of an agent, but you're damn effective. Good luck to you. I'm sure we'll be in touch when the hearings start to roll around."

"Umm, thanks, I guess? You aren't gonna try to hug me or make out with me right now or anything, are you?" Heaven forbid I let things be serious for two minutes.

"You're an idiot. Keep it together and stay alive, huh?" He left it at that, spinning around and walking out, bumping into the doctor who was entering my overpriced hotel room.

Thank goodness. "Perfect timing, doc. Let's get me outta here already."

Chapter 3

I spend another two months of my life in a rehab hospital outside Rough River Falls, re-learning how to walk and use my right arm. It's essentially a nursing home for people who aren't geriatrics. I'm eager to get out of here and get back home, although milking my injuries for everything they're worth with Kayla has made my recovery tolerable.

"What's your plan when you get outta here?"

"I haven't given it much thought, to be honest. I've been more focused on learning how to function like a human again. If I'm not mistaken though, I think the town could use a good mechanic." Of course I know I'm not mistaken. I'm directly responsible for the town not currently having a mechanic, what with Griz, the prior gearhead, being locked up behind bars thanks to me. "Seems like a natural fit to me. The only thing I understand more than law enforcement is the inner workings of a gasoline combustion engine, ya know? The one thing my dad did right was teach me a very useful trade skill."

"Why don't I come over there and you can get *my* engine running?" She saunters over to the door and gently latches it before strutting to the chair I'm currently occupying. She plants her knees in the cushion on either side of me and straddles my lap. Luckily, *that* part of my anatomy was left unscathed following my accident...ifyaknowwhatimean. Wink, wink, nudge, nudge.

A tapping sound comes from the door. Of course it does. Kayla climbs off of me at the sound. Dammit, doc.

"Yeah, come on in," I call, irritation dripping from every word. The door swings open quickly, and just as fast, a masked man in a leather vest is bearing down on me from across the room. Thanks to my injuries, my reflexes are damn-near nonexistent aside from my sweat glands and heart rate, which isn't useful in the least bit. What am I supposed to do here? Sweat on the guy until he submits? He crosses the room in four steps and raises his right foot to deliver a front kick toward my head. His boot lands squarely on the chair back cushion, centimeters from my face.

Kayla has an even slower/worse reaction than me, and she just now decides to take action by bolting for the door. My assailant orders her to stay put and she obeys. What the hell, Kayla?! The guy peels off his mask and exposes his stupid face – Scott.

"Dammit man. The joke's on me, I guess."

"Had to see how your recovery's coming along," he states. "Are you gonna be able to handle people's shit when you get outta here?"

"Shouldn't need to. Hasn't Kayla said anything to you?" I ask.

"She's said a lot of things to me. She's my sister."

"Ugh, you're such a smartass," I accuse him. "About the DEA and my recent unemployment?"

"Of course she told me," he concedes, glancing over in her direction. "That was like, months ago. Which brings me to the reason for my visit. This whole thing wasn't completely my own idea."

"So you're telling me that you had help putting together this little charade of a room invasion? I'm shocked," I say, rolling my eyes.

Scott turns toward my open room door and in walks an older, heavier set man. I've seen the guy around town over the last several months since my return, but I'm having a little difficulty placing him.

"Will, it's good to see you," the gentleman begins. He approaches and extends his hand. "Bill Williams. Town Manager for Rough River Falls."

It finally dawns on me. I'm talking to none other than Bill Williams. Town Manager for Rough River Falls. Okay, hold on. His name is William Williams?! Come on, you gotta be kidding me here. I stifle a little immature giggle and try my best to keep my composure and a straight face. "Regular visits from the DEA and now I have the Town Manager coming to check on me? I'm feeling a little extra important now."

"Speaking of the DEA, obviously we're all well aware of your recent exploits. Your return to town, the investigation into the Kings, the pending legal cases, and so on. Your presence has been very disruptive to our mild ways of living."

"Well, to be fair, your 'mild ways of living' included harboring an outlaw motorcycle club that was responsible for extortion, drug trafficking, the overdose death of a state representative's kid, aaaaaaaaand, oh yeah, murder."

"And your actions have gutted our town's identity and its ability to sustain itself. Before this conversation devolves into a finger-pointing competition, let me get to the point."

I shift my weight in the chair, intrigued by what is about to happen.

He resumes, "There are some very ugly truths that we have all been forced to face in the last three to four months. The bottom line is this: the town is imploding, Will, and at this point it's unsustainable. Put your feelings and opinions of the Kings aside for a minute and listen to me. Twenty-five guys were arrested and removed from a population of only 412. Arresting six percent of the town isn't a drop in the bucket and it goes far beyond a small ripple effect. That's a tsunami-level event we're talking about here. And when the tidal wave came crashing down, it destroyed everything in town in its wake. Griz's Garage shut down since the proprietor and half the employees are now incarcerated, but that leaves the other half of the mechanics who are still around and now out of work. Rusty's Tavern is now struggling since a lot of their most loyal patrons are locked behind bars. The library is closed because El C's old lady was fired and not replaced. Theft is on the rise because people are desperate to make ends meet, and petty street crime is escalating because the Kings aren't around any longer to deter it."

"Well damn, Bill. That's a pretty grim outlook. And you've seen all of this in the span of three to four months?!"

"Will, we're talking about a working-class town here. Pretty much the entire town lives below the poverty line. It's not like there's money floating around for people to build savings accounts for a rainy day – much less a torrential downpour like now."

"And I'm sure you didn't come down here to throw stats around about just how much I've ruined Rough River Falls," I conclude.

"Not at all. I can see why you were so valuable to the DEA. You've got a good head on your shoulders. Will, I need your help. The town needs your help," he pleads. "The town council has approved the creation of a position of one town marshal."

"And you want that to be me," I finish for him.

"I do. You are hands down the only qualified candidate in town."

"Bill, look at me. Thanks for the offer, but I'm still learning how to walk and write my name. You want me to chase punk kids and cocaine tweakers, then write up a shit-load of paperwork about it? I'd love to be able to help, I really would, but I simply can't do it physically," I confess.

"Just think about it Will. Myself and the council are all well aware of your recovery and we aren't willing to fill this position with just anybody. We're eager to have somebody in place so some semblance of order can be restored to the town, but we are more than willing to wait for the right person. That person is you. Take care of yourself and get outta here soon," he states, turning toward the door to exit my room.

I look around the room to the faces that are still present. First to Kayla, who looks back at me with a blank stare. She clearly wasn't anticipating this conversation. Then I move my gaze to Scott, who's nodding his head.

"Do it," he encourages.

Chapter 4

I vigorously shake out my clothes as I take them out of the dresser and refold them to fill my suitcase. That's right, folks…I'm going home!

"Guess who came into the tavern the other day during my shift," Kayla asks, giving me a few seconds to consider my answer.

"Hmm. Scott?" I ask half-heartedly.

"Mr. Williams," she responds.

I stop folding my clothes. "That was my next guess, of course." She's got my full attention.

"You're an idiot. He asked if you've given any thought to his proposal."

I slightly nod my head a couple times. "And what am I supposed to patrol in? My pickup?"

"That response right there isn't a 'no,'" she points out. "You should talk to him."

Dammit she's smart. We finish gathering my belongings before a staff member rolls me to the front door in a wheelchair, a small box of personal affects in my lap. Kayla follows with my suitcase in tow. We reach the exit and the double doors automatically slide apart. Wouldn't you know it, the one and only Bill Williams is standing outside next to a damn nice four door pickup truck. "What's he doing here?" I mutter to Kayla out of the side of my mouth.

"How else were you planning on getting home? Did you expect me to borrow Scott's scooter?"

"Will, it's good to see you! You're looking well," Mr. Williams says as he approaches. He extends his hand to assist me out of the wheelchair.

"Thanks. So is your truck," I reply.

"Ya think? Well thanks. I'm a little fond of it myself if I'm being honest. Let me help you get loaded up and we'll get you home, sound good?"

"Sounds very good. Let's do that." Bill takes my belongings and gently places them in the bed of the truck while Kayla escorts me to the passenger door of the vehicle and steadies me as I work my way up into the leather seat. The three of us get situated in the enormous pickup, then Mr. Williams expertly navigates it out of the parking lot and toward Rough River Falls.

"Will, it would probably be a good idea to discuss some things before we get to your apartment," Bill starts in.

I can see Kayla in the side mirror, gazing out of her window while this discussion takes shape. "You don't miss a beat, do you, Bill?"

"Well first of all, I just want to warn you a little more of the state of the town before we get there. Ya know, try to ease the shock a little bit for you."

Gee, how thoughtful. "Thanks, but I'm a big boy. I can handle whatever fallout there may be from my actions against the Kings. I'm sure you're itching to get down to business and make your next sales pitch to me about why I should be your Sheriff."

"Town marshal," he corrects.

"Potayto, potahto. Who gives a shit?"

"The Grayson County Sheriff's Department for starters," he points out. "You will be a recognized officer of the law, but you will not be a Sheriff's

Deputy."

"Right, that would involve giving me a cruiser," I mumble just loud enough for him to hear. "Speaking of which, in this little fantasy of yours, what do you see me patrolling the town in? I have a bike that's unrecognizable as a motor vehicle of any kind and a beat up old pickup that I can barely count on to start when the temp drops below forty."

"We've been offered an SUV through a local dealer who has also agreed to outfit it with all the equipment you'll need. There's nothing like a tight-knit community that you can count on for support in a time of need."

"That's a helluva gesture," I acknowledge. "So let's say I agree to this disaster of an idea. What kind of timeframe do you have in mind before I'd be on the streets?"

"Obviously, that would depend on your recovery and physical state, Will. As soon as you're ready to go."

I check the side mirror again and Kayla's gaze is still fixed on the horizon. She's mindlessly nodding her head. It seems to me like everybody has been having conversations without me, and arrangements are being made without my say so. Can't say that I'm too thrilled about that, since it's gonna be my ass on the line. A quiet falls over the cab of the truck for the remainder of the twenty minute drive back to town.

Mr. Williams breaks the silence as Highway 54 becomes Main Street and the speed limit drops from 55 mph down to 35 mph. That, my friends, is the very definition of a speed trap. I can only imagine that's how a lot of my upcoming time on duty will be spent; hiding out behind a bush and pulling over unsuspecting passersby to hand out citations.

"Will, I feel like you should know that things aren't quite the way you left them. I just don't want you to be too shocked by what you see when we get to your apartment," he warns as he turns off of Main Street.

I'm not too sure what I'm getting into, but I gotta admit, I'm a little worried with that kind of build-up. We pull into the parking lot for my apartment building and I spot my pickup right where I left it…just not quite *as* I left it. First, I notice that the axles are sitting on concrete cinder blocks instead of round chunks of rubber commonly referred to as tires. I slide out of Bill's cab as soon as he comes to a stop and I step directly toward my truck. As I approach, I notice the driver's side window is broken in and the hood isn't latched. I lift the hood and immediately notice the glaring absence in my battery compartment. After a quick once over, it doesn't look like anything else is missing. I check the passenger side and notice that the glove box was rummaged through. All my paperwork and napkins seem to still be present, but my flashlight and breath mints are gone. What kind of monster steals a man's breath mints?!?

After taking inventory of the damage to my truck, I turn my attention to my apartment. Dammit. As if I wasn't already pissed off enough about my pickup. My eye is immediately drawn to the black spray paint adorning the red door of my domicile. Three capital letters spell it out as simply as possible – PIG. From there I spot the plastic covering the front window to my living room. Something tells me that wasn't put up to help with insulation purposes. I slowly approach the residence, push the door in, and survey the scene. My place has been completely ransacked; the TV was thrown to the floor, my beloved movie collection tossed around all willy-nilly, and my furniture is shredded. "Good lord. Is this ground zero for where the zombie apocalypse started?? I just always assumed it would originate somewhere in El Salvador or something." It doesn't look like I was robbed, but rather somebody really wanted to get a message across. The black spray paint on my red door might be more than sufficient evidence of where I should start looking.

"Tell you what, Bill. Get me a light bar and a laptop for my truck, and a radio so I can communicate with the local sheriff's department and other local law enforcement agencies. I'll handle the installation and repairs on my own."

"That isn't asking much, Will. We can certainly acquiesce to those requests," replies Bill.

"Well now I didn't say I was done," I shoot back, almost cutting him off in mid-sentence. "You aren't getting off that cheap. All the money I just saved you will have to be reallocated in my budget."

"What are you thinking?" he inquires.

"Obviously, I'm gonna need a bike."

Chapter 5

Knowing that he would get the desired reaction from me by taking me to my apartment, but also knowing I had no place to stay until things were cleaned up, Bill ends up driving Kayla and me back to Main Street and dropping us outside Rusty's Tavern. That isn't technically the name of it, but the local bar and grill had changed owners and names so much in the past twenty-five years that the residents just reverted to calling it by its original name and stuck with it. Anyway, I digress. The small diner serves as Kayla's source of income, as well as her residence. The property houses a small one-bedroom apartment above the tavern, which Kayla occupies. And now, I suppose I'll be occupying it as well for a while. I sure hope Kayla's cool with that.

As soon as we get my things out of Bill's truck and upstairs into Kayla's apartment, we settle into her couch and start making out like a couple of high schoolers. Finally, we can act with no fear of being interrupted by nurses, physical therapists, or doctors. As I'm sure you can imagine, before long, we were beyond making out...again, just like a couple of high schoolers.

We make our way back to the tiny bedroom and I lay her down all romantic-like. Well, as smooth as I can for still relearning how to use my limbs. I lay down beside her and hear the creaking of her front door opening. "What the Hell?!" I blurt out. As quickly as possible, I get to my feet, make sure all of myself is covered up, and storm from the room to confront the intruder and defend my lady's honor. "Dammit, Scott. Could you possibly be any more annoying?" I ask, more than a little serious.

"Just thought I'd stop by for a little bit. Ya know, be your one-man greeting party. Maybe talk some club business while I'm here." Scott interrupts the bedroom action to talk about the Kings?! Not cool man. He must sense my hesitation and irritation with his next line. "Hey, once a King, always a King, right?" he asks.

"Right, about that. Maybe you're forgetting how the club voted me in after making a drug run for them, then voted me out all in the span of a week and a half. Not sure your 'Once a King, always a King' mantra rings true."

"Yeah, well, I didn't forget about that, but this is a new era for the Kings."

"Why are you so hell-bent on keeping this club alive??" I ask exasperatedly.

"Because it's all I've got!" he spits back. "This is what I know, and this is all I have in my life besides Kayla. I need this," he trails off.

Ugh. Dammit, kid. "Two guys don't make an MC, you know?"

"Does it matter if there's three?"

"Who the hell else have you convinced to waste their time pretending-" then it hits me. "Jaws?!?"

"You know it!"

He's the only other person affiliated with the former Kings that didn't manage to get tangled up in my bust, but he was only a "hang-around" at the time. Not even an official prospect yet. "Good lord. I don't even know the kid's name. And there's no damn way I'm calling him Jaws."

"Will, we aren't changing our road names."

"You can't be serious. Scott, they called you Junky for Christ's sake,"

I remind him. "Why would you want to keep that label and be reminded of those asshats and what they put you through? And don't think you're gonna keep calling me Legacy. I don't really need that reminder of my swell ol' dad."

"You can't change your past, Will. And if you try to forget it and ignore it, then you're bound to make the same mistakes."

"Whoa. That's deep, Prez."

"Shut up, asshole."

"I'm still not calling you Junky."

"There's no way in Hell he's calling you that," Kayla interjects from the doorway to her bedroom.

"Then call me Prez," he offers, flashing that shit-eating grin of his.

"Come on, let's be serious here for a minute. I get that you want-err, *need*, this club to keep going, but you don't even have a bike," I point out, matter-of-factly.

"Well yeah, there's that," Scott acknowledges. The final act of indignity that the club bestowed upon Scott when they voted him in as a full-patch member was gifting him with a scooter. In normal situations, that might be seen as a rather generous act, but in the motorcycle world if you're on a scooter then you might as well be a smashed pile of dog shit on the side of the road. "Lucky for me, with you being out of commission, that opened up a bar-tending gig at Rusty's, so I've been doing that for the last few months."

Upon my return to Rough River Falls, I took a part-time gig tending bar at the local tavern to give the appearance that I wasn't an undercover agent. Always gotta cover your tracks, ya know?

Scott continues, "You're right about me not having a bike, but I'm working on it. I've been able to save a decent amount of money between paydays, and Kayla has let me crash on her couch since the clubhouse was demolished, so that helps." The DEA tore down the former clubhouse following my sting. They wanted to make a statement, and also didn't want to leave any remnant of the club behind. Unfortunately, the one kind act the club ever did for Scott was letting him shack up in a backroom of the clubhouse while he prospected. It kept him close for them to torment, and it also gave the Kings a live-in maid to clean up all of their messes.

I slowly start to nod my head as the realization settles in; there's no room for me here. With Scott sitting in the lone recliner, Kayla pads her way over and squeezes next to me on the couch. Kayla must sense where I am mentally. "You can crash here for a few days. Until your apartment gets cleaned up at least."

"Thanks. I'll call the landlord and see if they have any other open units I can move into to try to expedite the process," I mention. "Let's go back to the clubhouse for a minute," I redirect the conversation back to Scott. "Where do you plan on the club meeting, Prez? In addition to actual members, a meeting place is also a pretty basic requirement for a motorcycle club."

"I might have something in mind," he responds. I can sense his frustration is growing. "You know what? Forget it. I was hoping you might have some insight. Maybe even be a resource to help me with this, but all you wanna do is poke holes in everything I'm trying to do. Screw it man, I'll figure it out on my own."

"Shut up, Scott," I fire back. My frustration kicks in as well. "Yes, I'm poking holes in your ideas because your plans are so damn flimsy. You want to keep a club going that literally ruined your life. On top of that, you're

trying to build it from the ground up because guess what? All the bikers in this

town are locked up. You can't have a club without members. And the cherry

on top is that there isn't even a clubhouse. You're missing the very

fundamental elements of an MC. I never said I wasn't in, I'm just pointing out

that it's going to be an uphill battle."

I see the hint of a smile form on his lips. "Alright," he says

sheepishly at first. I can see the enthusiasm growing. "I have something to

show you when you're ready." With that, I stand up and walk down to the

tavern. I can already tell I'm gonna need a drink or seven.

Chapter 6

The next few days are spent going through the wreckage in my apartment and trying to clean and organize all of it. My landlord wasn't too keen on giving me another apartment while all of my belongings still occupy that disaster that was once my home. Plus, at this point, I'm a bit of what you might call a pariah. Nobody in town has been overly helpful since my release from the hospital aside from Bill Williams. And his help has only been based on getting me up and running to ensure his property stays safe. My progress would be pretty minimal due to my injuries if not for Scott being so willing to lend me some normally functioning hands. Gee, I wonder what *his* motivation is to help me so much.

"So when do you think you'll be up to checking out my idea for the clubhouse?" he begins non-chalantly. Wait, what's the opposite of non-chalant? Chalant? Because that's exactly how he's been since I woke from my coma at Grayson County Med Center. That boy has a one-track mind, and I've heard nothing but that one track every second he's around.

"How 'bout after I get to sleep in my own bed for one night?" I shoot back. I'm feeling more than a little testy at this point. Scott's hounding me about the club and helping him with that, Bill Williams and the town council are hounding me about getting the town marshal office operational, Kayla's concerned about Scott and wants me to keep him from doing anything to hurt himself, and hell, I'm just trying to function like a normal human being.

"Alright, take a breath. I wasn't trying to twist your panties up in a bunch. "

"Dammit Scott. Get it through your hard-boiled head. This club is gonna take time. It's a process to get organized and get the wheels moving on something like this. We have no clubhouse. We have no members. And neither of us even have a bike. Even if I did have a bike, there's no way I could ride it. I'm getting damn tired of pointing this out to you over and over and over."

"And I'm well aware of all these things, Will. You aren't the only person telling me how this is a bad idea and how it ain't gonna work. Frankly, I'm fed up with people fighting me on this. If you're with me, then good, let's do it. If you aren't, then fine. I gotta get to work. My shift starts in 20 minutes." With that, he leaves me standing in a heap of broken dishes in my kitchen.

I spend a couple more hours shifting things around my humble abode until there's at least a foot path that I can tight-rope walk from room to room, and I think I finally have all the broken glass vacuumed up from the floor...I think. I hope. I crash down on my sofa and fight to wrangle my cell phone from my pants pocket. If I was smart, then I would've pulled it out before I sat down. If. As you may already be aware, I don't generally do things that are all that smart. In a rare stroke of brilliance, I start scrolling through my contacts until I find what I'm looking for, then hit that little green circle to initiate the call.

"Yeah?" comes the voice from the other end, somewhat out of character.

"Hey, it's McGee."

"No shit. Caller ID, numb-nuts. What do you need?" He cuts

straight to the point.

"I heard some things, so I wanted to go straight to the source to do my fact-checking."

"Is that right?" he inquires. "Tell me what you've heard and I'll tell you how much of it is bullshit."

"Word on the street is you're getting out." Silence screams from the receiver. "I was wondering what your plans are." I try to keep my tone flat rather than lilting into a question at the end. I want him to know that I have good sources and am well-informed.

"Don't really have any. I honestly haven't given it much thought," he states. "Why?" he asks again.

"Listen, bottom line – I need your help," I state matter-of-factly.

"I'm in. Once my discharge comes through I'll be there."

The call disconnects and I relax further into my couch. Exactly as I expected; no questions asked and no hesitation. I wasn't excited about resorting to that, but I already know the assistance will be more than necessary. I will myself to squeeze in a nap, which wasn't all that hard since my body was sore as shit from working around my apartment.

*****

I awake a couple hours later, sore and grouchy as all hell. I have a nagging and inexplicable desire to talk to Scott. On the bright side, my left leg has fallen asleep and is currently in the pins and needles stage. Even better still is the fact that Scott is at Rusty's and I have no mode of transportation, which means I'm about to hike my grumpy, disabled ass a few blocks down the street. Before setting off on my adventure I try to convince myself that the exercise will serve as some much-needed physical therapy.

I hobble my gimp ass downtown and try my best to stroll casually into the tavern. I've gotta be careful and not lead on that I'm in as bad of shape as I am. I need to keep appearances and not let on to the town folk that I'll be anything less than effective when it comes to policing the community.

I spot Kayla floating across the dining room with a tray full of dirty dishes propped up on her shoulders. Hmm, how 'bout that. She has shoulders. Guess I never noticed that before. I mean, I assumed she had them, but I always focused on other areas. Now that I'm paying attention I can't help but notice the elegance of her shoulders. Everything about her screams femininity. And I mean that in a positive way, not a chauvinistic way. The first part, about looking at her other assets was totally chauvinistic, but I'm not completely sure I needed to point that out.

I glance toward the bar and spot Scott washing some glasses at his work station. He sees me and nods an acknowledgment, so I walk in his direction. "Hey shithead. We need to talk."

"Is that right?" he asks. I can already tell he's gonna enjoy this a whole lot more than I am. "Am I supposed to assume I know what you're referring to? You know what they say when you assume- you make an ass out of Uma Thurman."

"You're an idiot." If dry sarcasm doesn't fit a particular situation, then my fallback go-to is mean-spirited name calling.

"You know, you're gonna have to start showing me some respect if you're on board with this. With me being your Prez and all." Oh yeah. He's definitely gonna enjoy the hell out of this.

"I'm in. And I have some ideas, but I need one thing from you, Scott."

"Name it," he says, a little too cocksure for my liking.

"Patience. I need patience."

He nods his head.

"Come talk to me after your shift," I conclude the conversation. He might think he's the Prez, but he better know I'm running this shit.

Chapter 7

I hear a knock on my door early the next morning. I've already been awake for a couple hours, but I'm not sure what normal person would come calling this early. Especially since everybody in the town hates me except for three people. I grab my pistol just to be safe before checking the peephole in the door to assess my visitor. My grip tightens on the firearm. Of course, it's one of those three people I just referred to. If it had been somebody that visited my place while I was in the hospital, then I highly doubt they would've knocked. I crack the door open. Scott's standing there with a bag of donuts from the gas station.

"You're up early," he comments through the slit in the door.

"Yeah, well, when you've been in a coma for the better part of a month there isn't a lot of sleep to catch up on. Besides, if either of us are up early, wasn't it you that just closed the bar last night? Let me guess, you couldn't wait to sit down and talk?"

"Hey guy, you're the one that came to me last night, remember? You also told me to come see you after my shift, so here I am. And I brought a surprise."

Immediately my door slams into me, knocking me off balance and sending me stumbling back into the living room of my apartment where I further trip over a rolled-up space rug and land square on my ass. My mind is reeling just as bad as my feet as I try to figure out what the hell just happened. Apparently, there's somebody else on the other side of my door that I hadn't even seen yet. Good lord I'm an awful detective. I roll to my stomach and awkwardly push myself back to my feet as quickly as I can…which isn't that quick. I pivot on my back foot to try to create as much space as possible between myself and my assailant. I bring my hands up ready to throw as I turn to face…Jaws?! He approaches me briskly. I'm unsure what's happening and why, so I hold back my aggression. He doesn't. He throws a stiff left jab that I absorb with my forehead. Before I can shake off the shock he grabs my shirt with both hands and gives me a shove, right over that same carpet that I tripped over about four and a half seconds ago. Ugh, I really gotta move that damn thing. I scurry back to my feet and bull rush him before he can apply any more offense. I take him down to the floor and mount him like I'm some kind of trained cage fighter. I cock my right arm back for the one-hitter quitter, but I'm interrupted by the sound of chuckling before I can deliver the blow.

"Get off me dick," Jaws spits out between laughs. "You passed."

"I passed?"

"We were curious what kind of progress you've been making with your recovery, and Jaws was more than happy to volunteer, you know, because of your history and everything," Scott explains.

When I first got back to town fresh from my separation with the Air Force, I was hanging out at the local garage trying to endear myself to some of the brothers. One night, while I was working on fixing up my dad's old bike there was a visitor. Me and one of the Kings chased the kid down and we smashed in his face, crushing his mandible. That visitor eventually came to be known as Jaws.

"What's up, Jaws? Get up, grab a seat." I clumsily collect myself, standing and stepping to the side. "Watch your step and try not to damage anything. You break it, you buy it."

"Damn, looks like I missed a helluva party," Jaws quips as he takes in the sight.

They carefully make their way to the couch and I grab a seat in a folding chair normally reserved for my small dining table. And by "small dining table" I mean a fancy(ish) folding card table. Ah, the extravagance of the bachelor lifestyle. Well, might as well get to it, I suppose.

"I assume Jaws is up to speed with everything?" I ask. I can't fathom the idea that Scott hasn't crammed this idea down Jaws's throat too. "And also on board?"

"Yep," comes the simultaneous response from the two stooges. So eloquent and well-spoken.

"Alright, listen up. We have three members and zero bikes. This is the shittiest MC of all time." Jaws parts his lips to speak up, but I continue my monologue without letting him interject. "I've reached out to somebody about giving us a hand. He's not from here and he's not available to get here quite yet. Let's just say he has some time to finish up before he's a free man." I can tell that I have their full attention. "All you need to know right now is that I trust him with my life and I'd be more than willing to give mine for his. So now we're up to four, but it's gonna be a few more months. Oh yeah, I forgot to mention that he rides, so that's another plus. Now let's hear what you clowns have been able to come up with."

Jaws cracks his mouth to finally be heard, but Scott cuts him off. "Well we all know that the clubhouse was demolished by the DEA after the bust to send a message. The good news is they didn't destroy everything. The garage and shed that were along the side of the property are still standing. By my guess, that would be more than adequate space to turn into a new clubhouse."

"Who owns the property?" I ask.

"The club owned it, so as far as I know the club still owns it. Not sure whose name was actually on the property deed, but I also don't really care. The clubhouse has been on that property forever. Either the landowner is dead or one of the idiots you locked up. Besides, who's gonna say anything about it?"

The glory about outlaw organizations is there isn't much of a paper trail. "Refresh my memory. How big are the buildings?"

"Two and a half car garage and the shed is big enough for pretty much whatever you want to use it for; you could throw a motorcycle lift in it or a pool table, run plumbing and turn it into a kitchen/bathroom, or even better yet, a bar. Pretty much whatever you could come up with."

Intriguing. Promising. "I don't know about you assclowns, but I'm no plumber. Or any type of laborer for that matter, and those guys don't come cheap. Any ideas on how to bankroll this little venture?"

Jaws finally gets to butt in. "I might." He's a little timid. His voice barely reaches me from across the room. You can tell he's not used to being involved in this type of setting. "We should go for a ride first," he suggests. "My car is out front, so I guess I'll drive."

"I know me or Scott ain't driving, so yeah, I guess you are."

We stroll out to his car in the parking lot. Late 90's Mercury by my guess. Not really the kind of car you would picture a young guy driving around in with his buddies. Oh well, who am I to judge? It's a vehicle, so Jaws is producing more for this club right now than me or Scott. Scott tries to call shotgun, but with one quick glance he changes his mind. Like I said earlier, he might think he's the Prez, but we all know who's running this show. We all pile in, me sitting shotgun and Scott sitting in the back and before you know it, Jaws is turning onto Clubhouse Road. That right there should tell you how integral this club is to this town. The damn road is named Clubhouse Road, and it dead ends right where you would imagine. Jaws pulls onto a grassy patch where the Kings of Chaos clubhouse once stood. The whole street looks different without the sizeable structure dominating the end of the drive. Over to our right are the buildings Scott had mentioned back at my place that were easily overlooked when the house was standing.

We begin walking toward the garage as I continue to survey the scene. The first thing I notice would be easily overlooked by a civilian. Bullet holes in the aluminum sheet metal of the structure screamed for my attention. It didn't take much effort to re-create their origin in my mind. After a several-month-long investigation and infiltration into the Kings, it all culminated with a showdown on the clubhouse lawn. Scott was nearly caught in the crossfire, and I was damn lucky to avoid the direct line of fire which was aimed at me with very bad intentions. You don't typically double cross an outlaw motorcycle club and live to tell about it. Huh, maybe I'm not that bad of a detective after all. I managed to single-handedly subdue three full patch members all while I was unarmed. Sounds kind of unbelievable, doesn't it? It was like a page right out of a book, and a poorly written one at that.

Jaws peeks in a dirty, smudge-covered window as Scott reaches for the door. He wraps his hand around the knob and gives it a twist. The door sticks a little at first, then I see him give it a little shove and it opens wide for our entrance. Scott looks at us and gives a little shrug. As we walk in, I fully expect to find folding tables set up with beakers and burners and pots strewn about. You know, your typical layout of an abandoned meth lab. I'm not shocked when none of those things occupy the space though. After all, I'm fully aware that the basement of the local library is where the club operated its enterprise. The garage is dusty, but barren otherwise. Clearly excited, Scott speaks up. "What do you guys think?"

Jaws peeks at me, then looks at Scott before answering. I cut him off. "Yeah, this'll work out nicely," I confirm. "A broom, dustpan, few cans of paint, and some furniture will do wonders. The question now then is where do we come up with the capital to get up and running?" I've got a decent income from the stipend I receive from the government due to my injuries happening while I was on their payroll, but it's hardly enough to bankroll this whole operation. Obviously, Scott has no resources buried in a mattress anywhere, and given Jaws's car outside, it's probably safe to assume the same for him.

"Let's go for a ride," Jaws mutters, his speaking voice totally taking Scott and me off guard. I also couldn't help but notice that he still can't seem to fully open his mouth. Yikes. And I thought *my* recovery was slow going.

"Where to?" I inquire.

"I have a proposal," comes his response.

I'd be lying if I said that my curiosity wasn't piqued.

Chapter 8

After the short drive out of town, Jaws makes some twists and turns, leading us even further into the middle of nowhere. I see his head shifting as his eyes scan his mirrors, surveying his surroundings. It's a very discreet thing to notice, and to see a civilian acting that way makes me nervous. I sit up a little straighter in the passenger seat and begin trying to locate what has Jaws so uneasy. As I'm quietly checking the mirror on my side of the car, he veers abruptly off the road. "What the hell, man?!" I blurt out before he pulls the car behind a stand of trees, out of the sightline of passing cars. My palms get clammy and I begin cracking my knuckles. I really hope he isn't having ideas of retaliation for his mandible. Move on already, amiright?

He kills the engine with the flick of his wrist and swings his door open. He slides out of the driver's seat and walks around the front end of the car. Scott and I watch him in silence. Well, I assume Scott is watching him. He's sitting directly behind me, so I can't really be sure what he's up to back there. I'm probably giving him way too much credit by assuming that he's noticed the same things that I have. Jaws jerks his head to the side, encouraging us to follow him. Sure, why not?

Scott and I hustle out of the car and step quickly through the weeds to catch up to Jaws. "What in the blue hell are we doing out here other than getting eaten by chiggers and ticks?" I ask.

"You'll see in a minute, don't worry," Jaws utters. "And it would probably be good if you kept it down. You never know what you might rile up out here."

After several more minutes of walking through the woods, Jaws points out a makeshift lean-to mixed in amongst the trees. "Hang tight right here, I'll swing around and see if anybody's home." He steps through the brush silently and is out of sight on the opposite side of the structure in no time flat. Scott and I are looking at each other, waiting for some kind of signal on what to do next when I hear the unmistakable sound of a revolver hammer cocking behind me.

Dammit, I'm awful at this, I think to myself.

"What the hell do ya think yer doin'?" comes the question from the armed stranger.

I slowly turn my head and catch a glimpse of the very definition of a mountain-man. This guy stands about six foot even, and weighs in probably somewhere around two sixty-five. He's got an impressive beard that would make any ZZ Top fan jealous, and he's wearing blue jean bib overalls with a flannel shirt that has the sleeves torn off. Hell, add a piece of straw dangling from his mouth and a lip full of chewing tobacco and this feller would have been a real-life cartoon character.

"Who are ya and why're ya here?"

"Yeesh, slow down with the questions," I pop off. "We haven't even answered the first one yet."

"Awful mouthy for somebody staring down the barrel of a .38," he points out.

"Yeah, that's probably my best quality." Good lord, I've gotta get myself under control. You'd think somebody as mouthy as me would have giant cojones. If only. That's Spanish for testicles, by the way.

"Scott, what are you doin' out here?" he asks, shifting focus.

"Honestly, I'm not real sure," Scott answers earnestly. "He's with me though," he states, nodding in my direction. With that, the pistol is slowly lowered until I'm no longer in the crosshairs.

"Dad, we need to talk," comes Jaws' muffled voice from behind us as he rounds the corner of the small building. "I have a proposal."

"Oh, you're the idea man now?" his father spits back. "I can't get any help from you when I need it, but now you wanna swing by the still-site with some strangers and call all the shots?"

Did we just walk into a one-sided Hatfield's & McCoy's situation here, minus the McCoy's?

"I get it, you do all the cooking, then I show up for the payday. We really don't need to rehash it again. Before you start in on me for the millionth time, this is different." His dad lets his silence respond for him. Jaws continues, "I know you hate running the deliveries and making the drops. You're more comfortable hiding out in the woods brewing up your latest recipe, hiding in the trees. Well, we'll make the runs for you."

Umm, did Jaws just rope us into bootlegging?! The stupid look on my face is verbalized by Jaws' dad.

"Why? What's in it for you?"

"We need some capital. We'll inherit the risk of getting busted if you're willing to cut us in on the profits."

My throat finally agrees to join the conversation. "Jaws, what are we talking about here? What are we running?"

"Moonshine, ya dumbass," the old guy chimes in.

I'm not used to being on the receiving end of sarcasm. "Yeah, I got that. What kind? If we get pulled over, I need to know what color it is and what it smells like so I can come up with a plausible excuse."

"Well this is Kentucky, son. It's pure corn whiskey. I cut it down to a hunderd proof so it's a nice drinkin' whiskey. That's what my buyers want, so that's what I give 'em. If you want some tutti frutti apple pie peach infused sissy shit then I would advise you make a trip to the North Carolina border and see what you can scrounge up." Condescension drips from every word.

"What kind of arrangements do you already have in place? How many buyers? Frequency and locations of the drops? Do you deal face-to-face or do you rely on the honor system?" My mind kicks into gear sorting out details and necessary strategy to take on this endeavor.

"You sure got a whole lotta questions for somebody I don't trust," the brew master replies, squinting his eyes and glaring at me.

"You bet your ass I do! I need to know what kind of risk I'm going to be submitting myself to. You guys know I'm supposed to uphold the law, right? Not willingly break it?" I see the old guy bristle at my mention of the law. I probably should've realized he doesn't know who I am, so finding out I'm the sole local lawman likely isn't going to endear me to him any more than my charming personality.

Scott finally decides to chime in. "Littering is illegal too, isn't it? But when was the last time you heard anybody getting stopped for it?"

Point taken. I see the old guy still hasn't relaxed about me being an officer of the law. "Don't worry, old-timer. If the only officer in the area is on your payroll then you don't have to worry too much about getting busted, I guess, huh?"

"Unless you're tryna set me up. I know who you are, son. I know you're not loyal to anybody but yourself."

That last comment hits home and stings, but it's hard to argue against. I know what the Rough River Falls public's perception is of me and I don't have the time or energy to try to plead my case here. "I've already seen everything I would need to if I had any interest in what you're doing out here. If you can't trust me, then trust your son." And with that, I suppose I'm about to start running 'shine.

"The local folks I ain't worried about. I'll make those deliveries and handle the transactions. You don't really need to know everything I have going on," the old bear of a man states, looking me square in the eye. "I'll give you the risky runs. That's what you're offerin', ain't it?" Well, yeah, I guess it is. "My big money comes from across the border. The bulk of my product is distributed in Tennessee. You're more than welcome to take those runs."

Gee, thanks. How generous. Transporting illegal liquor across state lines. Well, at least it isn't drugs again, I guess.

"What's all this about anyway?" he asks, turning his focus to Jaws. "Why this interest all the sudden?"

That's an easy one, so I interject. "This town has a legacy to uphold. The Kings might be locked up, but that patch is ready to run. It's expensive getting things going, so we could use the help."

He chortles at the thought. "So you jackasses wanna play dress up and act like big, bad, tough bikers? Dumbasses," he trails off.

Scott jumps in this time. "Nobody's playing dress up. Will's been around the Kings his whole life and was the first legacy full-patch member. I was voted in before the bust, after spending years as a hang-around and prospect. So you can think what you want, but you might not want to say it out loud." I see a little fire in his eyes and I'm more than a little impressed. Although, the negotiating table isn't really when you typically want to get testy with people. The old guy glares at Scott in response to the tense exchange. Scott ends the conversation with a final instruction before turning to walk back to the car. "Let Jaws know when the shit's ready to go. We'll take it from there." Damn, kid. Way to hold your own.

As we begin tromping through the weeds, I quietly hear Jaws make one final request to his old man. "Dad, I'm gonna need to get those keys from you."

Chapter 9

The next couple weeks are spent getting my pickup back in working order. Since somebody was kind enough to get my wheels and tires out of the way, I decided to go ahead and install a four-inch lift kit to the suspension before throwing on some beefy, off-road rims and rubber. I cleaned the rat's nest out of the air cleaner and replaced the battery, slapped a wench on the front bumper and then vacuumed out all of the shattered glass fragments from the passenger compartment. I replaced the catalytic converter that went missing while I was away, then sent it off to the nearest garage for the final touches.

When I got it back, the windows were tinted, a remote start and lo-jack tracking unit was installed, a light bar was bolted to the roof, and it had been given a paint job and decal package to identify myself as the fuzz. They also hooked me up with a spotlight on the driver's side. This truck turned out pretty badass, if I do say so myself.

All the tooling around on the truck also served as some pretty serious and highly effective therapy as well, as it helped rehab my fine motor skills. It was also during this time that I was given a key to my office by Mr. Williams. Turns out, the town took over the property of the old bank and since it already had a vault in it, they just swapped out the solid steel door for something with bars. It really was a lot more space than what I needed, but I sure wasn't going to complain. Hell, maybe I could use the space to host some support group meetings – you know, after I sell them the hooch, then they can come on down to my jail and talk about how they can't stop drinking. Is that unethical? Hmm, who knows.

More important than getting the keys to my new office, was the other conversation I needed to have with Mr. Williams, centered around getting another key. "Bill, I'm impressed with the arrangements you have provided for me, and not to sound ungrateful but I just want to make sure that you haven't forgotten the rest of our deal."

"No worries, Will. I haven't forgot, and I am a man of my word. Having said that, I believe this is what you're referring to," he said, pulling a shiny key from his pocket with a lucky rabbit's foot keychain attached to it. He must notice the skeptical look on my face. "I'm sure you had your own ideas how this would go down, but I think you're gonna like what we were able to come up with."

"Bill, with all due respect, I'm unsure why you thought it would be a good idea to make this call without consulting me. A man and his motorcycle is a very intimate thing, and you can't just pick one out of a line-up. That's like walking through the state fair and just pointing at a woman for an arranged marriage. It just ain't gonna work out."

"Before you make up your mind that my taste isn't good enough, maybe you oughta walk outside with me," he assures.

Fine, I'm already here, I think to myself. What have I got to lose? Worst case scenario is they try to push a Ninja on me and I make them take it back to the drawing board with precise instructions on what to return with. Much to my surprise, when we walk outside and round the back corner of the building to the small staff parking lot, my eyes lock on a fully dressed cruiser. Sometimes referred to as a "bagger," this bike is decked out with a windshield, saddlebags, cruise control, and a trunk; all the bells and whistles you could ever ask for on a motorcycle. I immediately recognize the unmistakable long, sweeping lines of the gas tank – a signature look for any Victory motorcycle.

"What you're looking at is a gently used 2009 Victory Kingpin Tour," Mr. Williams confirms. "We don't have the budget to let you pick something out from a dealer, but we've been keeping a very selective eye on the nearby auto auctions. Go ahead and try it on. See how it fits," he encourages.

"Don't mind if I do." I step next to the bike and swing my leg over the saddle before sliding down into the seat. I can't resist admiring the two-tone paint job; the deep burgundy contrasting beautifully with a light gray. I stand the bike up off its kickstand with ease. I can't believe how balanced this machine is, and for the first time in my life, I'm speechless.

Mr. Williams must recognize the look of awe in my eyes, and coaxes me along to further explore the bike. "Fire it up," he eggs me on and I oblige. The engine fires with no effort, pulsing out a very muted exhaust note.

"Well that's not gonna do," I muse to myself. For the first time since I spotted this beauty, something finally missed the mark. I see Mr. Williams's expression shift from pleased with himself to curious about what the issue was. "You know what they say – loud pipes save lives. I'm gonna have to drill the baffles out of these pipes."

Mr. Williams chuckles. We are both well aware that I was sold on this bike the second I got the key, it just took me a few minutes to realize it. Now that I'm already planning my first modifications, this thing has finally found its rightful home.

I flick my left leg back, swinging the kickstand up away from the ground and carefully begin to walk the bike backwards out of the parking space. "Whoa, where are ya heading?" Mr. Williams questions. I give the engine a couple revs and act like I can't hear him over the low rumble. "We still have a lot to figure out inside, Will."

"I have plenty to figure out out here," I reply. "Thanks for this."

"Well when are you coming back? Should I stick around?"

"Let's meet back here in the morning. Nine o'clock work for you?"

Surprisingly, he nods his head and doesn't try to argue. "See you then," he simply says, followed with, "Be careful on that thing. We both know what happened the last time you were on a bike."

That's a reminder I didn't need. I turn my head away from Bill to check the path in front of me. My nerves are on high alert. I can feel my muscles twitching and my legs are shaking. It feels like this is the first time I've ever ridden before. In a sense, it almost is. I just don't want anybody else to see me trembling, so I focus on steeling myself and keeping it all together. Very slowly and deliberately I start to relax the grip of my left hand, easing out on the clutch. Once I feel the engine start to engage, I begin to roll on the throttle in my right hand. The RPMs rev higher and the machine begins to roll away from our starting spot. My whole body is wound as tight as a rubber band until I turn onto Main Street and begin to run up through the gears for the first time. In the blink of an eye I hit the edge of the tiny town and I settle into a nice, comfortable cruising speed. I reach my right thumb over to the cruise control and engage it. Once that's done, I throw my feet up on the higher pegs. I pull my left arm off the handlebar and let it rest in my lap. I stretch back and naturally meld into the bike. My nerves disappear and take my fear with them. I haven't felt this relaxed in months.

That changes in no time. Within moments I find myself approaching the Highway 54-110 split, and can't help but notice my muscles tensing up on me again. My legs come back down to the primary footpegs without me realizing it. My left hand, filling with perspiration, finds its way back to the hand grip. Visions of my last trip to this area dance through my mind. My eyes lock onto the mangled guardrail along the side of the road. My shoulders and neck muscles are contracted so tight they could crack a walnut. This is the exact location that I nearly died. Following the shootout with the Kings of Chaos at the climax of my infiltration into the club, I was injured and riding this stretch of road leaving town when my body finally gave out on me. Without my faculties, I lost control of the bike, and well, you know the rest of the story.

In what feels like an eternity, I start to stand the bike up out of the curve. This thing is so incredibly balanced with its 100-cubic inch engine that I couldn't even tell I was in the middle of a curve. It could also have something to do with my brain being a little distracted. Regardless, riding this beast is effortless. Thank goodness for muscle memory, because my actual memories are trying their best to betray me. I resume my cruising position and don't look back. I haven't even checked the gas level yet. I hope there's enough to last awhile, because now I have no desire to stop. I cruise past the entrance to Rough River Falls State Park and lay on the throttle, sending the annoyingly baffled muffler into a low growl.

*****

After a long day of cruising the highways and back roads, I find myself returning to the town limits of Rough River Falls. I downshift and drop my speed to the posted 35 miles per hour. As I cruise down Main Street, I spot my destination and slow to a stop in front of Rusty's Tavern. I kill the engine and drop the kickstand before letting the bike come to a rest. I attempt to stand up from the saddle, but my legs are less responsive than a college student to an alarm clock. Fatigue has settled into my muscles from being so tight and constricted. I guess my nerves never went away during my ride like I thought they did.

I refocus and will myself onto my feet. Slowly, I force my leg up and over the seat to dismount. My hip screams at me and I can't contain a yelp of pain. I pivot and lower my leg back to the ground while glancing around the parking lot to make sure nobody was around to hear my audible instance of discomfort. Luckily for my pride, I was all alone aside from a couple cardinals in a tree along the edge of the parking lot.

I swing the bar's door open and stroll into the tavern. Controlling my movements as much as possible to mask my pain and inabilities, I walk to the bar where Scott is working. He looks up and tosses a nod in my direction. "See that?" I ask, casting my head to the side to indicate the bike parked out front. He nods in appreciation before making eye contact with me. "I'm back," I say with a shit-eating grin.

Kayla is working too, and she must've spotted me when I stepped in because she's already by my side. I lean over and plant a kiss on her in the middle of the dining room.

Yeah. I'm back.

Chapter 10

Let me fast forward a few more weeks so I can save you from hearing the boredom about getting my office set up. Unless you really want to hear about the installation of the jail cell door, and my preference on how I like the placement of my pens and stapler on my desk. I know, enthralling, huh?

These weeks also provided enough time to get the new clubhouse set up. I had fronted some funds for some minor construction; insulation and drywall inside the structure, a bathroom, small bar, and a soundproof insulated meeting room with double doors. We were able to procure a card table, pool table, and some decent furniture that wasn't too ragged from thumbing through trader magazines and perusing yard sales. Scott, being the delinquent that he is, even spray painted a pretty damn good Skull King logo on the exterior of the building.

Kayla was helping with the interior decorating to keep it from being a complete pig sty, and at least help us figure out the best layout for the space. She was pointing out where things should go and Scott and I were handling all the heavy lifting. While carrying a love seat from one side of the clubhouse to the opposite, a thunderous rumble rises from the distance. Scott and I lock eyes, curiosity being the prevailing thought. We drop the sofa from knee height and beeline for the door. Kayla had already hung some privacy blinds and curtains to keep nosy neighbors out of club business, but that also meant that we didn't have a clear picture of what was going on outside until we reached the doorway.

My brain didn't know how to process what was happening. I could clearly see that Scott was beside himself in elation, but I was in more of a state of disbelief. While a nice ride will often leave me speechless, this time my silence was caused by the rider. A clean, midnight blue cruiser pulls onto the property and parks directly in front of Scott and me. The rider drops the kickstand, kills the engine, and dismounts. Jaws looks at us, presenting the bike like he's a Price is Right model, and simply says, "Ehhh?"

"Hell yeah!" Scott blurts out.

"Nice, Jaws. Where'd she come from?" I ask. "Or do I even wanna know?"

"Don't worry, it's clean," he assures me. "This bike has been in the family since it was new, but it doesn't see much action since dad got involved in his outdoor activities. A bike isn't really good for hauling things, ya know? Anyway, remember when we talked to my dad last month? Before we left I let him know that I had some use for it and needed the key. A new battery and some air in the tires was all she needed, so here I am – ready to ride."

"Hell yeah," I echo Scott's sentiment, nodding in appreciation of the clean machine. "Tell us about her."

"'95 Kawasaki Vulcan 1500. Soft bags and straight pipes. Everything else is from the showroom."

"Damn nice, Jaws," I offer.

"Damn nice," Scott concurs. "Come on, it's about time we had our first official meeting."

The three of us wander back inside and head toward the far wall, where the meeting room was recently constructed. Scott reaches the double doors first, but waits for my hobbled ass to catch up. "I have a surprise of my own to share with you," he says, setting the tone. He pulls the doors open simultaneously, exposing the contents of the room. The surprise misses the mark on Jaws due to his unfamiliarity with the Kings' history, but the significance is not lost on me. Sitting in the middle of the room, dominating the floor, is the meeting table from the old clubhouse. There's nothing special about this table aside from just being a solidly built piece of furniture. What makes it special is its age. This is the first and only table to have official Kings business conducted at it since the original six founding members formed the club.

"I managed to salvage a little bit from the old clubhouse before the feds brought it down," Scott says, acknowledging my reaction. The comfy office chairs are gone, and there are only three folding chairs toward one end of the table. I notice that Scott was able to procure the old gavel as well, as I spot it lying at the head of the table as he approaches it. He invites us to take a seat before picking up the gavel and slamming it down on top of the table. "I couldn't wait to do that," he says like an idiot.

I take my seat on the side of the table to Scott's right, and Jaws grabs the chair opposite from me. "Let's get to it then," Scott begins. "I was waiting for the right time to do this, but I didn't really know when that would be. Seems that now is as good a time as ever." I cock my head slightly out of curiosity of what else he had in store for us today. "The rebirth of this club has obviously been my passion since the Kings disappeared last fall, and I've already made my claim on the President's seat. Any objections?"

None that were worth fighting over. "Nay," I say. Jaws follows suit.

"Will, you know more about the Kings than anybody else left in this town and I need your knowledge and expertise. I've already offered you to be my VP, and I think that would serve this club the best. Any objections?"

"Nay," comes the unanimous response.

"Jaws, that leaves Secretary and Treasurer duties for you. Since you're familiar with tracking income off the books through your dad's enterprise, I think this is a no-brainer. Any objections?"

"Nay."

"I was hoping this is how things would go," Scott comments, standing up from the table. He walks behind me, past the double doors, and steps in front of a familiar looking storage cabinet. I hadn't noticed it sitting in the corner of the room until now, but I instantly recognize it from the meeting room of the old clubhouse as well. Scott twists the handle and pulls the door open. I see a smirk cross his lips as he reaches inside and pulls out three leather vests, fully adorned with Kings of Chaos patches as well as patches denoting President, Vice President, and Secretary/Treasurer. He hands them out and we immediately put them on. "Will, I know you already know how to treat that. Jaws, I'll fill you in since this is the first time you've ever sat at this table. That vest does not leave your body unless you're taking a shower. Defend it with your life, and know that there are people who may test you over it."

Jaws nods, but I'm a hundred percent certain the levity of this moment is not sinking in with him, which is why people don't get patched into an MC until they've been put completely through the ringer during their hang-around and prospect periods. Potential members are fully tested during those periods for multiple reasons, but primarily to ensure they fit in with the brothers and for the club to know without a shadow of a doubt that when push comes to shove, they know that every member can be counted on.

"Does anybody else have anything to present at this time?" Scott asks. Jaws shakes his head.

I speak up. "Scott, we can't have a motorcycle club that anybody will take seriously when our president is riding around town on a scooter."

"Yeah, about that," he starts, cracking a shit-eating grin. He pulls a newspaper from his back pocket and tosses it on the table in front of me. It's folded to the classified section, with one ad in particular circled several times with a blue ink pen. It reads: For Sale – 1997 Honda Shadow American Classic Edition, 1100 CCs, wrecked once, gas tank replaced with matching tank from same year Honda Shadow Spirit. "Meeting adjourned. Let's go for a ride. I've managed to save some dollars from the bar and my time has come."

*****

Scott directs me through town as I chauffeur him around in my patrol truck. He barely looks up from his phone while he barks out driving orders. "Left here. Right after the church," and so on. It doesn't take long before we pull into the small parking area for Big H's salvage yard. Jaws trails close behind on his Vulcan, the exhaust note announcing our presence before we ever come to a complete stop. As I'm reaching for the door handle, Scott makes one more comment. "Go with whatever happens while we're here." I'm not sure what that means, but as long as he does then I'm fine with it.

We walk to the side of the shop, where Big H keeps his inventory of vehicles that actually run, and we immediately lay eyes on the Shadow. It sticks out like a sore thumb amongst the other well-worn, used vehicles which all happen to be four wheeled cages, or your typical car for all you civilians out there. It's actually a damn good-looking bike – white wall tires that flow right into the black and cream paint scheme, six inch pullback handlebars, leather fringe dangling from the clutch and brake levers, soft leather saddle bags below the passenger seat, padded sissy bar for the passenger's comfort, floorboards in the front and back instead of puny little pegs. Somebody made a small investment in this bike to customize it just right – chrome accents in all the right spots without being over-the-top, and just all around tastefully put together.

Big H strolls out to our group. He's wearing his typical carpenter pants and work shirt that's unbuttoned a little too far with his chest hair hanging out. The shirt has the standard name patch on the left side of the chest. Not his real name of course, but it rather simply says "Big H." Scott is inspecting every inch of the motorcycle from the ground up. "What do you think, Will?" he asks, looking for an expert opinion since he's never owned a bike of his own before. I walk around the bike, nodding casually. I smell a faint odor of gasoline, and see a stained trail down the side of the engine casing beneath the gas tank. The gravel is clean under the frame though, which is a good sign and tells me it's not a big leak and there's no sign of oil dripping from anywhere.

"Four grand," Big H blurts out without anybody asking, flashing his best used car salesman smile. Too bad for him, his Indian corn teeth ruin any positive effect he's going for.

"Four grand my ass," is my blunt response. "It's leaking gasoline and it's a Shadow, not a Harley. You know you ain't getting four grand for an import bike this old."

"Exactly. It's a Shadow and not a Harley, which means it's reliable. The price is four grand."

Pointing out the shortcomings of Harley Davidsons isn't typically the popular approach, but he isn't necessarily wrong. While a Harley can be rebuilt and brought back to life from nearly any condition, they are a finicky animal. "Big H, you know you ain't gonna get four thousand dollars for this bike. Two grand, and we'll get it out of your way."

I can see him bristle physically at my counter offer. "Fire it up," he says, tossing the key *at* me, but not necessarily *to* me.

"So help me, if I go up in flames because of this piece of shit I'm never coming back here," I declare as I approach the machine. Scott drifts around to the far side of the bike, seemingly to get a good angle in case the bike explodes and he needs to bail. I slide in the key, open up the choke, reach across and hit the electric ignition, then jump back just in case. The V-twin engine rumbles to life with a great sound emanating from the exhaust. There's a lope, and you can hear the programmed timing from the Honda factory to give it an intentional miss in the firing cycle. That was done to try to replicate the signature Harley exhaust sound. Harley wasn't too keen on that, so they sued the shit out of Honda over it. Needless to say, Honda had a redesigned engine the very next year. I can't really say that I care much about all that though. As Big H mentioned, Hondas are reliable and this bike sounds great.

"The gaskets were a little dried out when I first got the bike, so when I put gas in it, some of it ran out here and there. It seems the gaskets have come back around after soaking up some of the fluid."

"Well you just said it, Big H. There's work to be done on this thing.

I'll give you twenty-five hundred, but that's it."

Big H apparently takes offense at my counter offer. Without any warning, he springs to his left and grabs Jaws' right shoulder with his oversized mitt. He pushes Jaws back as he sweeps his leg forward and Jaws immediately hits the gravel. Jaws rolls to his stomach in order to push himself back up from the ground. I start to make a move, but that's when I make eye contact with Scott and he winks at me. Our brother is getting his ass kicked and Scott effing winks at me! Then I remember what he said when he got out of the truck – just go with it.

"You stingy bastards stop in here and low ball me right to my face!" Big H yells while clawing at Jaws' back. "Gimme that vest, boy! I'm gettin' me a souvenir today so everybody that stops by here knows right up front not to screw around with me!" He gets a grip of the vest around the shoulders and starts to yank and rip at it to slide it down off Jaws' arms. Jaws regains his balance and locks his hands together in front of his stomach to keep the vest from being taken off. He twists abruptly, breaking Big H's grip, and pulling him slightly off balance. Jaws shoves Big H to gain some space, then charges the big junker and tackles him to the ground. Jaws sits up on Big H's torso in a full mount position, ready to rain down some blows when Scott steps in and breaks up the melee.

"What the hell, man?" Jaws asks as Scott is pulling him off Big H. Big H makes his way back to his feet, while Scott calms down Jaws.

"Calm down, you passed. Don't worry," Scott tells him. Jaws lets his guard down, but casts a quizzical look toward Scott.

"It's called a mudcheck, ya dumbass," Big H informs Jaws. "So people can see how well you hold yer shit together."

"I know what Will is all about. He's been around the club and the military his whole life. I have no question about his dedication. I just wanted to see how you would react when push came to shove."

I could see Jaws shake his head at the notion of his loyalty being tested. "That's how it goes Jaws. You kinda had the fast track, so I think this was pretty much necessary," I state, agreeing with my Prez.

"Alright, twenty-five hundred," Big H concedes. "Cash," he clarifies.

"Of course cash. Scott, pay the man," I instruct before Scott pulls out a wad of money and counts out twenty-five hundred dollars in mixed bills. It takes a while because of that. It also takes a little longer because Scott isn't the brightest bulb in the house. He's killed plenty of brain cells with his checkered past. There's a reason all the old MC brothers nicknamed him Junky. Once he's done, Big H takes him inside to finish the transaction and retrieve the title for the motorcycle. Before I turn to walk back to the truck, I glance over into the salvage yard. Immediately, my eyes lock onto something eerily familiar.

My focus is broken when Scott trots back out and throws his leg over the saddle of the Shadow. He fires up the engine, then looks back over his shoulder at me. "You coming?" he asks.

"You guys go for a ride. I'll catch up to you. I need to check something out." My gaze returns to the junk heap. Without even realizing that my legs are moving, I slowly approach the mess that had full grasp of my attention. I reach my hand out to touch it, but can't quite bring myself to make contact.

I hear a noise from behind me. Big H had snuck up on me, and didn't seem sure if he should speak up or not, so he scuffed his foot on the ground and cleared his throat to let me know he was there. "Tough to stand there and take that in, huh?"

"Yeah, you could say that," I acknowledge, my voice trailing off.

Before me sits the wreckage of my dad's old Harley. Now, don't be confused just because I mentioned my dad. The memories that are currently haunting me don't have anything to do with him. The bike just happened to be his and I inherited it when he died. We had a very complicated relationship, and I'm being very generous by using the word "relationship." No, the thoughts running through my head date back to less than a year ago to when I last rode this bike. This is the machine that my life nearly ended on. I needed a minute to fully absorb the sight. The left front lower was ripped clean from the fork, explaining the absence of the front wheel and axle. The frame was mangled and bent in more directions than the Dragon at Deal's Gap. The rear wheel was cracked completely in two with the rear fender pushed up like a damn spoiler. The handle bars were pushed down so far they were embedded in the gas tank, which was also pockmarked with bullet holes from my last encounter with the original Kings of Chaos. How'd I survive that?!?

"Need anything else, Will?" asks Big H, breaking me from my daze.

"Yeah. Help me load up that bike."

"Uh, mmm, Will are you sure about that?"

"Yep. It's mine isn't it?"

"Well, yeah, I guess it is."

"Then I'll take it with me." Not exactly sure why, but I just need it in my possession. Hell, maybe I'll throw it in the clubhouse. Centerpieces are supposed to be conversation starters, right?

Chapter 11

By the end of the week I receive a phone call from a number that I don't recognize. I answer tentatively and hear Jaws' voice on the other end of the line. "Ready? It's time for a run. Meet me in the woods," he instructs. Luckily, I'm an observant person, and trained to always be aware, so I remember exactly where he means when he says "the woods."

Within twenty minutes I'm pulling my truck off the shoulder of the road and behind the stand of trees that Jaws used for concealment the last time we were here. Instead of stopping there and hiking though, I decide to drive a little deeper into the brush. Ah, the benefits of being a truck owner. Also, I have no interest in muling jars of moonshine back and forth from the still site to my vehicle. That's dumb and I'm too lazy for all of that nonsense. I've also decided that instead of trying to be sneaky and come up with plausible excuses, I'm just going to use my patrol truck. No cop is going to pull over another cop. And if somebody stumbles across me in the act then I'll just act like I'm following up on an anonymous tip and making a bust.

Once we get all loaded up, I start getting some details. "You got a few thousand dollars' worth of hooch back there, so be careful and don't cost me any money," Jaws' old man starts in on me.

"10-4, old-timer. You can save all of the dad speak though. Now where am I headed?"

"I got a buyer down in Tennessee, just across the border. Take US-79 South, enjoy a nice casual drive, and make some money."

"Simple as that, huh?" I ask, with no effort to mask the sarcasm.

"It's a dead drop, so yeah...simple as that," he states matter-of-factly. "And I trust my buyers. More than I trust my partners at this point," he says defiantly.

Knowing it's a dead drop helps ease my tension a little since I won't have any face-to-face interaction with anybody. The buyer leaves a stash of money at a predetermined location, then the seller swaps out the cash for liquor. With no inter-personal meeting, there isn't much risk about the buyer being a narc. However, there's always a chance that you're walking right into a trap, since the timeframe is pretty well determined at a set location, so it's not hard to organize a choreographed sting operation. The part that makes me more uneasy than anything else is the mention of crossing the border. Leaving the state in my marked cruiser could raise a few eyebrows. The only thing I have going for me is that it just so happens to be my personally owned vehicle, so if anybody in Tennessee law enforcement wants to get too worked up about it then I'll throw that out there and let them deal with it. Still, I feel uneasy about breaking the law through so many jurisdictions. And let us not forget that crossing the state line makes this a federal offense.

On top of all of that, as you may recall, I have some questionable history in Tennessee. It was right outside Clarksville, that I made a delivery of a different kind when I was infiltrating the Kings originally. I know, there's a whole lot of backstory in that one sentence. Well keep up, because you're about to get some more. The Kings had me running cocaine to earn my patch. My assignment was to deliver a backpack to a real winner of an individual named Dirty Mike in exchange for an identical backpack, presumably containing payment. Turns out, he doesn't like being called Dirty Mike to his face. It would've been helpful if someone would've told me that before-hand. You live and you learn though, I guess. Anyway, the drop turned quite contentious, with Dirty Mike and his goons trying to ambush me and keep both backpacks for themselves. When I managed to get away with the money bag, they attempted to run me down in an old Mustang while I was on my Harley. Yeah, not really a fair fight now, is it? Once I returned to the Kings and relayed the rundown of events, then President Riot made an executive decision to send a message, loud and clear, to Dirty Mike that that type of behavior simply would not be tolerated. So a handful of us rode back down to Dirty Mike's trailer, knocked on the door, and proceeded to murder one of his guys. There was a little more to it than that, but now you have the Reader's Digest version of what transpired the last time I entered the Volunteer state.

Now that we're all up to speed and on the same page regarding my uneasiness, my stomach continued to tighten all the way down US-79. I remember that there was a gas station on the Tennessee side of the border, so I pull off the interstate and make a quick stop. I top off my gas tank just to be on the safe side, then drain my bladder. Having one of those tanks full is good, having the other one full is bad. Always remember that, kids. It also gives my nervous system a chance to calm down, and it actually seems to help. At least until I get back in my truck. Once I climb back behind the steering wheel, everything reverts to being wound tighter than a spring. I pull the hand-written directions from my pocket and review them for the first time. Now that I've crossed the border, it would probably be helpful to know where I'm actually going. The further I read down the list, the worse I feel. Exit onto US-24 West followed by a couple quick turns down tiny, barely-there side roads. I break out into a cold sweat. Jaws' dad hasn't listed road names, because in all honesty, the roads may not even be named. But as he has described where to turn, I can visualize exactly where he's talking about, and I don't like it one bit. He mentions landmarks that I recall vividly from my last two trips down here. He has me pass an all-too-familiar RV park and campground, but I'm relieved when his instructions tell me to continue on past the entrance to the trailer park where Dirty Mike was holed up. Before I get a chance to breathe a sigh of relief though, I turn onto a gravel drive that's kind of hidden around a blind turn. Evidently there's a hollowed out dead tree that is supposed to have some cash in it, and that's where I'm supposed to leave the shine.

I clumsily slide out of the truck, as my motor functions still aren't what they used to be, plus my legs are asleep from being cooped up in my truck with only a brief break at the gas station. As I'm reaching into an empty knot-hole in the side of a tree, hoping that I don't get bit by a squirrel or bat or something worse, my fingertips graze something. My arm recoils in instinct, but I go back for a second feel to be sure I've found what I'm looking for. Luckily, I don't end up with rabies from any vermin, but I do end up with a fat stack of cash. Now I've gotta unload all this hooch.

As I'm carrying the last load of liquor from my truck to the tree, I look to my right and can make out the first row of trailers from the trailer park. Just past those is where Dirty Mike resides. Maybe I should go say hi? We could reminisce about the good ol' days – you know, when I could still walk like a normal human being and he still had a full crew. Nah, on second thought, I'm not convinced either of us is up for that. I can't help but wonder though, if this delivery might be more directly connected to Dirty Mike than I'd like to think about. I mean, he had his drug connection through the Kings, and it wouldn't be surprising if connections were made through them with Jaws' dad, given how small, tight-knit communities work. For somebody to get one hookup from another hookup isn't unthinkable. And when both hookups are small-time enterprises, you can kind of begin suspecting how this is gonna turn out. My thoughts spiral out of control the entire drive back to Rough River Falls from the dead drop. I have so many questions that need answered, but there are so many answers I don't want to hear.

*****

Back in town, I meet up with the other Kings at the tavern…just like old times. I slide into a chair next to Scott facing toward the front door. My training is so ingrained at this point that I'm not even conscious of my thought process. It's just natural to always select a seat where my back is least exposed and I have a clear view of doorways so I can monitor who's coming and going. Scott and Jaws are both wearing their vests. Mine is stashed back at my apartment just in case there was some type of turbulence on my run. Having any type of conflict wearing my vest, while driving my marked patrol vehicle, while bootlegging moonshine would be a tricky situation to work myself out of.

Kayla must've seen me walk in, because right after I take a seat she fills the last open chair at the table and flashes a grin in my direction. I may have actually just heard Scott's stomach churn. I'm sure seeing his sister flirt with his VP can't be much fun for him. Luckily for me, I don't mind.

"Hungry?" she asks. "Thirsty?"

"You know I'm always up for a sweet tea," I answer. "And let me get a beef Manhattan too. I built up an appetite on my trip." She stands to go put in my order and quickly leans across the table to give me a kiss before scurrying toward the kitchen. Man, she's great.

After our victory dinner, we drop off a cut of the cash to Jaws' old man. He seems somewhat pleasantly surprised to get his money without having to leave his property. His surprise could've also been because I didn't handcuff him at any point, which is probably along the lines of what he had in mind. With his gruff exterior though, I could have just completely made up his reaction because that's what I expected. Either way, run number one is in the books and now the club has a little spending money.

Chapter 12

We're flying high for the next several days; feeling pretty good about getting the club off the ground and back on track. Wearing the King's colors around town is starting to feel normal again. Once I returned to town after my bust, the thought of sporting the Skull King logo felt unnatural – especially given the fact that I essentially single-handedly dismantled the club. We spend a Saturday afternoon cleaning up fallen branches and debris following a fierce storm at the small town park. We follow that up by painting over some vandalism at Rough River Falls State Park. Technically, the park falls outside the town limits of Rough River Falls, but it still falls under the club's territory, and nothing is more important to a motorcycle club than territory. Well, maybe loyalty. It definitely comes down to territory and loyalty. And possibly discretion. Or respect. I'm certain one of those four is the most important thing to a motorcycle club.

As comfort starts to settle in around me, the guys, and the club, we find ourselves relaxing at Rusty's for another dinner meeting. And this is when it all comes to a screeching halt. Or, depending on your perception, maybe this is where it starts to get good? Hell, you be the judge.

So Scott, Jaws, and I gather around a dining table in the bar area of the tavern. Dirty dishes and empty glasses litter the table while we talk about our newfound budget, and how best to apply the finances to the club. Scott wants to put it into the clubhouse, make some renovations and dress it up real nice. Jaws wants to split it three ways and use it however each member sees fit. Personally, I just want to sit on it for a while, let it build interest, and see what else we can come up with. Reimbursing myself would be alright too though.

The jingling of the small bell attached to the door grabs my attention from our current conversation. As you'll remember, I always sit with a clear line of sight of the entrance/exit of wherever I am. Old habits die hard. This particular habit was instilled so that *I* don't die hard. Scott and Jaws were yammering on about why their idea was the best, when they both finally noticed my complete lack of interest in whatever it was they had to say. The look on my face must've been more expressive than I normally like it to be, because both of the knuckleheads spun around to scope out what my eyes were locked on to. Before they could make the connection, our guest was already at our table.

"Well look at you scumbags, sittin' here in public with those colors on, pretendin' to be big, bad bikers." He pulls no punches with his opening salvo, flashing a grimy, shit-eating grin. Recognition settles in quick for Scott. As far as I know, Jaws has never had the pleasure of interacting with this POS before now.

"Oh hey. Long time, no see," I say cordially. "Dirty Mike, is it?" I know full well what his name is, and I also know how he takes offense to being called by his informal nickname. I see him try to mask his reaction, but I can still clearly make out his body physically bristling at my cheap attempt to get under his skin.

"Yeah, it's still just Mike, dick."

I see hatred spark behind his eyes. He attempts to regain his composure as quickly as it faltered. "I just had the uncontrollable urge to confirm my suspicions of what's been going on up here in Kentucky. Ya see, I was keepin' my eye out for the latest shipment of my beverage of choice, when I just happened to glimpse an eerily familiar face."

I knew it. Hell, I called it. Even if my joints creek too much these days, that doesn't mean my instincts aren't still sharp. Seriously, scroll back like three pages if you've already forgotten.

"Anyway," he continues. "You don't forget the face of a man who's responsible for the murder of your best friend."

Geez, guy. Flair for the dramatic much? Well, on second thought, I guess he does have a valid point. It was my trial run that ultimately led to the early demise of one of Dirty Mike's guys. But still, it's not like I pulled the trigger or anything. Am I minimizing my role in removing a human life from the face of the Earth? I think I should feel bad about that. But it's really easy to justify losing one more coke addict from society. It seems like I should feel worse about that. Hell, even if I felt a little conflicted about it. What does that say about me? Did the MC change me this much over the course of the past year? Or maybe my upbringing caused this lack of empathy. Or maybe I'm prejudiced against people who try to double cross me. Or maybe the moon was perfectly aligned with Saturn. Who knows? I might just be a bad person. That could also have something to do with it.

"I gotta tell ya, after scopin' the dead drop and seein' yer big dumb face, I damn near put a bullet in it. But then a realization hit me. I'm gonna let you keep makin' my deliveries. You're on my payroll. You work for me now."

"Calm down, Dirty. This is no different than the arrangement you had with Riot and the other Kings. We're no more on your payroll now than we were then. We provide a service, you provide the cash. The clerk at the Gas N'

Go doesn't work for you just because you buy a gallon of milk, so stop trying to think before you hurt yourself," I respond.

"Yeah, if anything we work for my dad," Jaws interjects. Dammit Jaws, shut your mouth before I break it again. Don't give this bastard any personal information!

"Whatever you gotta tell yerself to fall asleep at night," he says, winking at me.

My stomach gurgles in disgust, so I belch in his direction. "Sorry, got a little queasy there for a second."

"Cute. Jackass. Just keep bringin' my hooch, delivery boy. And don't get any big ideas. I know ya have a badge, but ya can't touch me with what I know. So shut yer mouth and bring me what I want. If yer lucky, I might keep payin' for it."

I must've been too distracted with Dirty Mike, because I didn't even hear the bell on the door jingle when the next patron entered the tavern. Regardless, I couldn't miss it when the new guy stepped directly behind Mike and planted himself firmly to the ground, crossing his arms. Ol' Dirty must've seen the twinkle in my eye, or the fact that I couldn't hide my smile. My bemusement just irritated the hillbilly to no end.

"What's so entertainin', ya prick?"

"Oh, nothing. Just thinking about a conversation I had with a friend a couple months back." I take a peek over at Scott and Jaws to see if I can gauge their reaction, and it's precisely what I expect – utter confusion.

"Well, I just wanted to stop in and say, 'hi.' It's been too long, so I thought it would be good to catch up. See ya next week. But how 'bout ya just drop off the goods at my trailer. Y'know, for old time's sake." I can tell his sole intent here was to antagonize us, and taunt me in particular, which I'm sure he thinks he has accomplished. He begins to take a step back in order to leave, but his heel catches on the other customer's foot who was posted right behind him. Dirty Mike stumbles, falls into the stationary man, then bounces off and almost falls to the floor. "Excuse you, asshole," he says, trying to save face and maintain his tough guy façade.

"Excuse me?" the stranger asks, still occupying the exact same place and pose as before the contact. "I was just standing here. So excuse you then. Anything else you wanna say, or are we done here?"

"Whatever man. I got nothin' else to say," Dirty Mike picks himself and his pride off the floor, then tries to strut out of the bar like nothing happened. I just watch the scene in amusement as it unfolds. Once Mike is clear, I stand up to greet the stranger.

"Nice entrance," I begin, giving him a big bear hug. He reciprocates the gesture. I turn to face Scott and Jaws once we conclude our greeting, and the confusion is still locked on their faces. I point to the two sitting at the table. "Scott. Jaws. Meet Miller. This is my old Air Force partner and our new Sergeant at Arms. Any objections?" This is nowhere near typical behavior for a motorcycle club, but we're nowhere near a typical MC.

"Nay," comes the unanimous response. Hell yes. We're back. And our enforcer just walked through the door.

Chapter 13

After some celebratory drinks and general small talk for the guys to acclimate themselves to each other, we finally decide to call it a night. Last Call kind of helps us make that decision as well. Scott and Jaws each go their separate way, leaving me to escort Miller back to my apartment to crash. Luckily I have my truck parked in front of the tavern instead of my Victory. Making Miller ride bitch on the Kingpin doesn't sound like fun for either one of us.

We pull into the parking lot at my apartment complex, and I get a prime spot exactly one door down from my unit. I extinguish the headlights as soon as I come to a stop so they aren't shining on my neighbor's windows at four o'clock in the morning. We slide out of the truck and begin cutting across the small grassy area between the parking lot and my apartment door. We're still pretty amped up about the reunion tonight, so we're being a little louder than any reasonable person would appreciate, when my neighbor's door opens. She storms out of her apartment and marches directly toward me, slapping me in the face upon her approach. "Damn, sorry about the lights. I tried to turn them off before they woke anybody up!"

"You good for nothing swine! Thanks for screwing everything up! And why, pig? What was the point?" She yells at me. "And you think it's okay for you to wear those colors around, knowin' what you did to that club? To this town??"

Oh, right. She's mad about the other stuff, I guess. I manage to grab her wrist as her hand retracts from my face. With the shock of her slapping me still fresh in my mind, I'm honestly surprised my reflexes were that nimble. "Listen up lady. I did what needed to be done. The Kings were drug dealers and a kid died with their product in his damn vain. If you wanna act like I'm the bad guy because your trashbox of a boyfriend got locked up, then that's on you."

"My kid got taken away, and that's on you!" she interrupts.

"Good!" I fire back. "That kid is better off anywhere other than in your custody!" She tries to slap me again with her free hand, but she telegraphs it. I pull my head back and grab her left wrist with my free left hand. I saw that coming even if she *didn't* telegraph it. Ever told a mother that she doesn't deserve to have her kids? Even when it's true, no mother is going to idly stand by and let you get away with it. "If the only thing I did was get that boy away from you, then my job here was well done."

"You just don't get it," she accuses.

"Ma'am, relating to that boy is quite possibly the only thing I *do* get. My mom split before I was old enough to have memories. My dad was there physically but that was the extent of his parenting abilities, leaving my development up to my grandparents. I've seen you strung out, passed out cold in your apartment with a lit cigarette dangling out of your mouth while your son is outside, alone, unsupervised, wearing nothing more than a diaper. I have no idea who his father is, and I can only hope that you do. I sure as hell hope it isn't that sorry excuse of a former brother, Stitch. So where's the kid now?"

"Child Protective Services took him. He's with his grandparents," she says sheepishly. Irony at its finest. I can feel her aggression release from her body as the tension in her arms melts away.

"I'm gonna let go of you now, but before I do, hear this. I want you to go back inside and sleep this off. If you swing at me again, then I'm gonna haul your ass downtown and let you sleep it off in my holding cell. Understood?" She jerks her arms from my grasp, spinning around and walking away from me.

When she's back in her apartment, Miller speaks up. "Nice neighbor."

"Yeah, I'm pretty much living the dream here in this Podunk town with this one-bedroom apartment. Smartass." I jiggle the key into the deadbolt on my front door, cycle my wrist and swing the door open, presenting my extravagant living arrangements to my newest house guest. I shift my head from direction to direction pointing out the different rooms. "Kitchen, living room, pisser's over there, and my room is around the corner. You can crash on the couch as long as you need to."

"Gee, how generous of you, seeing as how I have nothing here and the only reason I'm here is because you asked."

"Oh, yeah, well, I'm glad you aren't gonna hold that over my head or anything." Miller is the only rival I've ever met to match my dry sarcasm, or as I like to call it, my undeniable charming wit. We get settled into the living room as he tests out his new sleeping quarters. I plant my ass firmly in my recliner after grabbing a couple cold ones from the fridge. "Last call my ass," I joke as I hand a chilled bottle to him.

We relive the showdown with the neighbor lady and all the things that I should've responded with, but wasn't quick enough to think of on my own at the time. You know how it is – you always think of the best comebacks and one-liners after the fact. Hindsight and whatnot. Kayla knocks on the door, then comes in without making me get up out of my comfy chair. She grabs a beer from the fridge, then joins me in my seat. Clean up at the tavern must've gone pretty quick tonight.

"I see you're wasting no time getting accustomed to life on this side of government regulations…that beard is coming in nicely," I comment to Miller.

"You know how it is. I'm letting my beard run free because the Air Force would never let me have one. I was never a fan of Mustache March. Besides, I'm not a used car salesman from the eighties, and the fighter pilots were the only assholes arrogant enough to think they could pull that look off."

Our conversation flows freely from one thing to the next as we get caught up with each other. I give him a rundown on the town, the club (both old and new), and my precarious position within each of them. He gets me up to speed with everything I missed after separating from the Air Force. "What's the story, man? How'd you manage to get here so quick? Didn't you still have another year on your commitment?" I ask.

"Yeah, give or take. Remember how I mentioned that my Pops was Air Force back in the day? Turns out he was part of the 82nd Combat Security Police Wing back in Vietnam. You know, all the guys that went through Ranger and every other Hua-Hua school you can think of. After you separated, my time came around to get into the 820th. It's a modern-day tribute to the Operation Safeside platoon from back in the day, only this time it was Operation Desert Safeside. Once my Captain found out about my ties to the original unit that spawned Task Force 1041 and my interest in following in my old man's footsteps, he made damn sure I landed with the new Task Force

1041. Well, shit happens and it turns out I didn't adjust too well coming back from overseas. Ran into some issues, and the Air Force and I agreed that I would be better off in a civilian role."

"Damn dude, that's rough. You must've gotten into some shit over there, I take it? Where were you, anyway?"

"Iraq. Stationed out of a joint base with the Army: Main Operating Base Balad/Camp Anaconda. My unit headed to town on an intel gathering mission. We came across some rumors indicating some insurgents were starting to form a camp, so we went in to check it out and put an end to it before it could get started. Once we got inside the town square, we came under fire. Nothing major, mostly just small arms. Amateur militia luckily for us. We hunkered down in the up-armored Humvees and let them absorb the rounds, keeping us safe from harm's way. Those things are basically tanks they're so heavily armored. As long as we aren't taking multiple rounds from a .50 cal or larger munitions like an RPG, then there's nothing to worry about. So we just waited out the attack. Eventually they either got tired of shooting or ran out of ammo. Once we had braved the storm, our intel gathering mission turned into a search and capture mission. We weren't willing to lose our foothold in this town to a camp of insurgents, so our new priority was to ensure the removal of as many fighters as possible. My team tracked a couple of the gunmen into a nearby house. We stacked up along the side of the door, getting organized and prepared to storm this residence."

The last thing you want is to enter an unfamiliar structure and have any confusion that could be prevented with a brief pause before kicking a door in. I never did a tour overseas, but that's basic common sense in our line of work. Miller goes on, painting a tense visual.

"I was the doorman," he continues. "I brought the sledgehammer and used it as my own personal skeleton key to get into any damn door I wanted. My job consisted of knocking the door in, then stepping to the side so the rest of my team could file in and secure the environment. I fell back in line at the end of the stack, and made sure there were no surprises on our six. Seeing the team operate was a thing of beauty. Groups of two would peel off and clear a room making sure there were no hostiles or threats while the rest of the guys breezed by them to continue clearing the structure. They were so well trained and in sync with each other, it was like they operated with one mind. There was never any question as to who went what direction and who took the lead at what point. I'm telling you, it was damn poetry in motion. So this particular place was one of the bigger structures in the town, and we were getting spread pretty thin as we worked our way through. I came up on a room that hadn't been cleared, so I checked it out. I stepped into the doorway and observed a Military-Aged Male at the opposite end of the room. He had an AK-47 hanging limp at his side. We made eye contact for a split second and I silently pleaded with him to stand still. Apparently our facial expressions didn't speak the same language because he didn't pick up what I was putting down. I raised my weapon and prepared to fire, but I got nothing. Not even the standard 'click' of a misfire. When my trigger finger found no purchase, I realized I was trying to aim down the barrel of my sledgehammer. He raised his weapon and prepared to fire, so I did the only thing I could. I flipped the sledge around, drew back, and took a full swing. Bo Jackson would've been proud. I made contact with the guy's temple, and his head just stopped existing. It splattered on the adjacent wall in a sickening mist. Chunks of bone, flesh, and brain dripped from my hammer. I managed to assist with the rest of the building, but that exchange took a toll on me. I really struggled to rebound from that. Taking a life in close-quarter combat is a whole different animal to cope with than ending somebody from long range in a firefight. After a couple weeks, it was apparent that I wasn't going to be able to continue my duties effectively, so I got shipped back home for a full psych eval. I managed to pass all the tests I was given, but evidently my behavior betrayed my mental capacity. After a couple traffic stops on base for DUI's and fighting with other Airmen, the Air Force concluded that I was no longer worth the hassle. So here I am."

Holy shit. I felt Kayla stiffen and shiver from the mental image. She stared at Miller blankly, her mouth agape.

"Damn man. I can't believe that. I don't even know how to respond. All I can even think to say right now is I assure you, this ain't that."

"It doesn't even matter. I don't really have anywhere else to be now anyway," and with that, he takes a long, slow pull from his bottle, sits the empty on the floor and stretches out on the couch, turning his back to us. Kayla and I take the hint and make our way to the bedroom.

Chapter 14

Kayla and I sleep until the crack of noon. We stroll out into the daylight streaming in through the picture window in my living room. Squinting, we both struggle to focus on anything. Luckily, vision isn't required to pick up on the smell of fried bacon. "Smells good," I mention. "Let me grab a plate."

"Better grab a skillet first," Miller pipes up. "What you're smelling is lingering from hours ago."

"Damn, what kind of house guest does that??" I ask incredulously.

"The kind that is left to his own devices for the first four hours of his first day in a strange, new land."

"Man, you're really just not gonna stop busting my balls about that any time soon, are you?"

"I've been here less than a day, so no, I'm not gonna stop taking these cheap shots until I get bored."

"Well *I'm* bored with it already, if that matters," I mumble loud enough for Miller to hear.

"Blah blah. Go clean your ass and get dressed," he instructs. "I got shit to do."

"Umm, you've been here less than a day, remember?" I remind him. "What do you possibly have to do that's so urgent?"

"Well, numb nuts, in case you forgot, I was voted into a motorcycle club last night. Kinda seems it would be good to, ya know, actually have a motorcycle. I need a ride to the nearest bike shop."

I nod my head. "Are you sure about that? We're in the heartland man. The nearest bike shop is a Harley-Davidson dealer in Bowling Green, about an hour from here."

"That sounds exactly like what I need. Do you know something I don't?"

"I know that a Harley should never be somebody's first bike," I state, matter-of-factly.

"Never speak in absolutes," Miller chides me. I'm not sure he caught the irony dripping from his own statement. "I'm American, Harley's American. Sounds like a good match to me."

"Sure man, that's definitely how you pick out a bike," I say as condescending as possible. "Do you even know how to ride?!" He looks at me and doesn't need to say anything. His mind is made up. "Get dressed then. Sounds like we've got an hour drive ahead of us."

All the way there, this asshole spouts off stupid, sarcastic questions in rapid fire. "How do seatbelts work on motorcycles? Do I have to keep my feet down when I'm driving, or how does it know to stay up? Do I get a helmet that matches the bike, or a bike that matches the helmet? Do they give me all of the Harley clothes, or do I have to buy that separately?"

"Yeah, don't. Don't be that guy," I finally chime in. "Get a Harley, fine. Just don't be a douche about it."

"Isn't that a requirement?" he asks.

"Well, yeah, valid question. But no. Just don't."

"Should I refer to the bike as 'my hog'?"

"I hate you," I trail off. Luckily, we pull into the parking lot before

Miller completely ruins my goodwill toward him.

The interaction with the Harley salesman goes smoothly with Miller calling all the shots. Without being familiar with Miller's background with bikes, I expected to have to be an active participate with the negotiations, but he surprises the hell out of me. He must've done some homework before he got here. That part doesn't surprise me. Miller researches anything and everything that he might need to know something about. Less than ten minutes go by with Miller chatting with the sales rep, and I see them wander off to grab a set of keys. I'm wandering around the clothing area when I hear a bike fire up. The engine revs a couple times, because c'mon, who can resist the sound of a Harley engine? As I'm taking in the sound of the engine, I hear it engage in first gear and accelerate. That's when Miller scoots by the front of the shop on a massive Heritage Softail Classic. He's gone for fifteen-twenty minutes tops, then returns from his brief test drive. While I check out the machine that caught his eye, he's already completing paperwork with the salesman. Before I even finish looking over the blue beast (the sales tag calls it Superior Blue – typical Harley mentality), Miller strolls back outside with the key and paperwork in his hand.

"Let's roll," he says casually, like he didn't just drop fifteen grand on a motorcycle in the span of forty-five minutes.

"Umm, yeah," I reply, taken aback with his adept purchasing ability. "All set then?"

"No, I'm stealing it and we need to get moving. Yes, I'm all set. You don't process information too quickly these days, do you?" he pops off. "And *I'm* the one with traumatic brain injury!"

"Yikes, guy," I respond.

"What? I'm allowed to say that because I have it. You're not."
Makes sense, I guess. "So now I got the bike. Where's the patch?"

"Slow down there, killer. Yeah, you've been fast-tracked into the club
based on me vouching for you, but you are in no position to get pushy. You'll
get your colors at our next meeting."

"Fine, let's go," he concedes. "I'd have you follow me, but I don't
really know the route so lead away. Just be sure to keep an eye on your mirror
in case I don't really know how to ride yet."

"Did I mention that I hate you yet?" I ask while climbing into my
pickup. "Sarcastic son of a," I trail off, closing my door. I take him the back
way home so he can get a good look at the country side and enjoy some of the
backroad twisties. What good is being on a bike if you don't enjoy the ride?
About ten minutes from town, my phone chirps at me. I look down and see that
I have a new message from Kayla. "Get to the tavern asap" it reads.

*****

I pull into Rusty's parking lot and see several of the regulars scurrying
outside. I throw my truck in park as my feet hit the ground. Hell, I'm not even
sure my truck came to a stop first. I bump into a few of the patrons on my way
to the door. Imagine a generic music video where the singer is walking against
the grain and he keeps hitting shoulders with everybody that passes him. That's
basically how it was playing out, except less musical. I grab the door to the
tavern and fling it open. The bells ring-a-ding-ding as I walk in, jostling them

when I jerk the door.

"You Junky?" I see a big brute of a biker reach across the bar and grab Scott by his shirt collar. One of his cohorts intercepts me before I can join the discussion. Another one of the visitors is banging a baseball bat against the edge of the bar. Louisville Slugger is my guess. After all, this is Kentucky. He's not hitting it hard enough to really do any damage, but it wasn't a light tap either. Basically, just hard enough to be effing annoying. "We heard some rumors about Kings colors bein' flown again down here. Thought it might be a good idea to get out and go for a ride; maybe confirm it for ourselves. Then sure enough, we walk in this shit hole and here's this asshole behind the bar with that Skull King logo on his back."

"Whoa," I speak up. Scott looks over at me. I can't tell if his eyes are full of fear or nerves, but neither one of them are gonna do him any good right now. "I'm not sure I appreciate you gentlemen coming into our town, running out all of our paying guests, then calling our citizens assholes and our businesses shit holes. I'd rather things start out a little differently," I attempt to calm the situation with my best qualities: wit, charm, and humor. AKA, sarcasm.

"Who the hell are you and why should I care?" the leader asks dismissively.

"I'm Will. Thanks for asking. And who are you fellas with?"

"It was a two-part question. Finish answerin' it," he instructs. Not much of a talker, I take it.

"Well the second part is a little more complicated. On the surface, I'm the VP of the guy you're about to rough up, and I don't care much for that idea." The guy that's standing directly in front of me, and between me and Scott, tenses up like he's about to spring. I twitch my head to let him know that's not a good decision.

The bells on the door jingle again, and the leader speaks up again. This time with even more exasperation in his voice. "And now who is *this* asshole?!"

I don't have to look to know that Miller was right behind me. "*This* asshole is our Sargent at Arms," I advise all of the strangers. "Looks like we have a party here now. But before anything kicks off, let me finish that two-part question. I told you who I am on the surface. But dig deeper and you'll find a badge." Playing the law enforcement angle with a group of outlaws usually won't get you very far. Luckily for me, I have an idea what they are doing here and I'm pretty sure they probably aren't in the mood for extra heat from the police. As expected, the tension quickly dissipates from all of the muscles in the room. Everybody has the understanding that going to jail isn't good for anybody.

The leader lets go of Scott, then turns his full attention to me. He casually struts over to let me know that he thinks he's running the show. I check the patches on his chest as he approaches and instantly spot the President patch right above the patch with his road name: Bruiser. Clever. He invades my personal bubble and looks me dead in the eye. "As far as we're concerned, the Kings died when the entire club was locked up. Bottom line – we've been talkin' about expandin'. Rough River Falls seems like a nice little place to set up shop." He looks around the tavern, nodding his head to his buddies. "Yeah, this territory will serve us nicely."

You see, territory is the number one concern for clubs. Well, right up there with respect. And a couple other things too probably. It's definitely in the conversation for most important concern anyway.

"We're not interested in patching over, but thanks for asking," I inform the mouthpiece for this club that's out of place.

"Well we weren't interested in bein' force-fed your cut of the business, but here we are. The Kings are gone. Dirty Mike ain't just gonna lose territory because some idiots can't smell a fed from a mile away."

Dirty Mike? "What Dirty Mike did with the cocaine after he got it from the Kings was his business. That doesn't have anything to do with us."

He laughs in my face. "That's cute. You think the Kings were the suppliers, and Dirty Mike was the dealer. How did you ever bust anybody?" he scoffs as he begins. "Wait, did you really think these inbred, backwoods bikers manufactured the cocaine in the basement of that tiny library? Man, you really are clueless."

The look on my face must relay the fact that I'm reeling from this revelation. My entire bust last year was based on bad intel. *MY* bad intel. I devastated my hometown, gutted its population, and ruined numerous families. Almost as quickly as the realization settles in, I dismiss it. This is no time to second guess myself. My bust was solid. I may have had the starting point of the drug ring backwards, but I had all of the right players.

"Dirty Mike wasn't gonna sit back and eat the loss of the territory and all of the sales, so he's been pushin' us to take more product. We've had to pick up all the slack you assholes created. Our market is flooded and our customers are tapped out. So here we are. You ain't keepin' up, so we're here to take over. Yer territory, customers, business…and patches. It's ours now. Everything."

I laugh in his face. "Listen. Bruiser, is it?" I ask as condescendingly as possible. "Bruiser," I repeat just for good measure and to be as irritating as I can. "Ima let you and your guys walk out of here now. *Right* now. We'll make it real peaceful like, and I'll even ignore the fact that you mentioned patching us over. That. Will. Not. Happen."

He chuckles. "Interestin'. You say some words and expect us to bow down. I may not know the Pythagorean Theorem, but I do know basic math, and the numbers are not in yer favor."

"You might be right assuming that you aren't dealing with the same ol' Kings, but I'm telling you right now, a hostile takeover is not in the cards for us New Kings, either. And let's talk about numbers for a sec." I reach into my back pocket and pull out my wallet, flipping it open to reveal my badge. "You might want to focus less on my patch and more on this shiny shield. You are absolutely right about me saying some words and expecting you to comply. You may have the upper hand in this room right this minute, but you certainly don't outnumber my partners in law enforcement. And if you make the wrong choice right now, then you'll never be able to outrun this badge."

"Calm down, Ponch," he says taking a half step back. Ponch? Really?? "I think we've seen enough here boys, let's get outta this shit hole." The rest of his club casually struts out of the tavern. Once he steps past me, I finally get a good look at the cut on the back of his vest. Bluegrass Bombers MC out of Owensboro. The stencil lettering is very distinct and has a military feel to it, which is fitting seeing as how this chapter was founded solely by

former military members. Well, as close to "former military" as the Air
National Guard will get you. The rest of the logo is just as subtle, with their
three-quarter skull wearing an old German helmet on top of a Maltese Cross
background. Their black, red, and white colors top off the Red Baron feel.

Similar to the Kings, the Bombers are an independent club consisting
of only the mother chapter. Unlike the Kings, the Bombers' base of operations
is much larger than Rough River Falls. Owensboro is just over an hour
northwest of Rough River Falls with a population of approximately sixty
thousand, making it the fourth largest city in Kentucky. Contrast that with the
blip on the map that is Rough River Falls, with its miniscule population of
about four hundred, and I start to wonder why Dirty Mike gives any shits
whatsoever about this barren area. Likely due to the more central location in
the state than Owensboro, I suppose.

After the MC rolls off the premises, Scott, Miller, and I stand still for
a brief moment unsure of what to do next. "Well, what now?" Scott predictably
asks.

"I would assume you need to finish your shift. Miller, you're with
me." We leave Scott to his business at the bar and make our way across Main
Street to the wanna-be town hall building.

We walk through the door and step to the receptionist desk. "What
can I help you with?" she asks absent-mindedly, not even glancing up from her
computer monitor. There are only three offices in the building, so I can't
imagine her work is that tasking or even engaging, really. There's the town
clerk, who keeps track of, you guessed it, clerical things. The treasurer has
their own office so they can keep an eye on financial matters, then there's the

other office that we stopped in for: the town manager. Essentially serves the same purpose as a mayor, but doesn't have the exact same responsibilities for a township that isn't incorporated. Blah blah blah, yada yada yada.

"I need to speak with Mr. Williams, please."

"One moment, let me see if he's available," comes her response. "Have a seat," she instructs.

I can see him sitting at a desk through the window in his office door, so I already know he's available, but I play along with the charade and sit in one of three chairs lining the wall next to the entrance. Miller grabs another chair leaving one between us. No reason to cram ourselves next to each other and not give ourselves any space. Plus, it would just be weird.

After a couple minutes, Bill finally walks into the waiting area. "Gentlemen, what can I help you with?"

Chapter 15

Once we get back to Mr. Williams's office I make introductions.
"Mr. Williams, Cade Miller. Cade, Bill Williams." I manage to get through
that without visibly snickering. The thought of this man's parents naming him
William Williams still cracks me up. Please let this be a lesson to any soon-to-
be parents out there. Don't make your kid's name a punchline. There's my
Public Service Announcement for this week. The more you know, right?

"Will, Cade, what can I do for you fellers?"

"Mr. Williams."

"Bill," he interjects.

"Bill, I have a request. Maybe more of a proposal, if that makes it
sound more appealing." His expression urges me to continue. "I think my
presence has started to have a small impact on street crime around here. I've
busted a few kids tagging buildings in town and let them know they aren't
gonna get away with it anymore. I've also raised some decent capital for
Rough River Falls through traffic stops for people speeding through town."

"That's hard to argue with, Will. Having the presence of an officer
and having people see your patrol vehicle around town has really curbed their
willingness to participate in thoughtless vandalism."

"Well, Bill. This is exactly what I expected. My immediate presence
made people second guess their mindless activities, so we've seen the short-
term drop in those types of crimes. *But*, I fear it's only going to get worse from
here."

"How do you figure?" he inquires. "People know they have

somebody to answer to now, why do you think it's going to get worse?"

Here's where I want to blurt out about the meeting that Miller and I just left with the rival MC, but now probably isn't the time to introduce that nugget of information. "Because the people that aren't really criminals that were partaking in the idiocy have been scared straight now. They aren't going to continue. However, the other folks that try to beat the system whenever they can are only going to try that much harder. They're gonna get a little sneakier and see how far they can push boundaries without getting caught. That's going to make my job a lot harder, and it's going to put the town at more risk. While these people are testing new practices, they're gonna try to come up with better laid out plans, more thought out crimes, and they're likely going to get a little bolder. They may take risks that Rough River Falls isn't used to."

"Isn't that a bit of a jump, Will?" he asks skeptically.

"It might be a small step, but it's really important to understand the new atmosphere around here. Before this past year, Rough River Falls had the Kings that kept things mostly in order around town. True, they created other problems of their own, but they also made it very clear that you don't screw around on their turf. That was one of the few perks of having the club around. They kept a little order around here before there was any police presence. Now they're gone, but I'm here. One man with a badge though, doesn't really have the same effect as a motorcycle club full of outlaws who are very stingy with their possessions."

"So what's your proposal then, Will?" he urges me to get to my point.

"One man with a badge? Ineffective. My request? Two men with a badge." Miller, who's had no clue what we've been doing here to this point perks up a little.

"Can't do it, Will," he responds. "There's no budget to double your department. You have to already know that."

"Bill, I'm asking for one more officer."

"Right. One plus one makes two. That's double. Are you gonna split your salary in half and pay him out of your own pocket? Will, your department, with you alone, makes up a fifth of our town's staff. If we add another marshal, then our police force would equal a third of our entire infrastructure. This is no police state. Aside from that, where are we supposed to come up with that kind of money?!?"

"I want you to think about something," I say flatly. I'm trying to reason with him without coming across as begging, but I also want him to know that this is something that I've thought out and not just some hair-brained scheme. "You came to me several months ago because the town is crumbling and you want me to help save it. You provide me a budget and some tools to be the lone officer in town. I can only work so many hours per day, so many days per week. There are a lot of other hours in the day when I'm not on duty. If you want me to help Rough River Falls, then give me what I need."

"Will," he begins. "You might want to re-evaluate which world you are currently operating in. This isn't your pretend-time, biker gang world. This isn't a shake down, and I'm not gonna stand here and let you extort me to get what you want."

I bristle at the mention of the phrase biker gang. We're not a gang and never have been – even before the bust when we wore the 1%er diamond patches on our backs. Outlaws? Perhaps. Okay, definitely. But the preferred nomenclature is Motorcycle *Club*. Write that down. It might save you a trip to the dentist if you ever find yourself in the presence of an MC. "Extortion my ass," I spit back. My response seems to catch him off guard. This is the first time he's really seen any aggression from me. "You want the town protected. Let me do my job and protect it the best I can. There are new threats that you don't know anything about. Let. Me. Do. My. Job." I look at him blankly. I'm not trying to intimidate him, but I want him to know that I am taking this seriously and I have no plans to back down.

He returns my gaze and slightly nods his head. "You're gonna have to bring in a lot more speeding tickets to pay for this."

On the way out, Miller whispers to me under his breath. "You could've at least given me a heads up about what we were doing here."

I look at him out of the corner of my eye and let a smirk smear across my face. "I think the words you're looking for are 'thank you.'" Man, it's been a busy day, but the good news is Miller now has a job and the Kings have just got a lot more back-up than we had before.

Chapter 16

Within days I have Miller outfitted with his uniforms, duty gear, and registered for his abbreviated police academy. Since we aren't a formal police department, we get the perk of fast-tracking our academy training. We aren't required to complete the full rigorous schedule of an accredited department. You know me, always a fan of the easy route. (Insert eyeroll here.) And in all honesty, police academy couldn't possibly throw anything at us that we hadn't already seen and conquered while in the Air Force. That's even more true for Miller than myself. The main difference is to shift our knowledge to local laws and statutes from the regulations we've been accustomed to while serving on military bases. That adjustment comes from sitting in a classroom with our noses in books, not doing pushup competitions with local meatheads.

As soon as he wraps up his classroom requirements, I have him start chauffeuring me around. Knowing the lay of the land could be the difference between being evaded by a speeder, and making the stop in order to bring in that sweet, precious revenue. If we were in a larger city I would say something more dramatic like, "Knowing the lay of the land could be the difference between life and death." But alas, this is the actual middle of nowhere and there's nothing like overstating the mundane.

Speaking of revenue, boy did we ever bring it in. Miller and I set up a rotating schedule to maximize the amount of time one of us was on duty. We set up a sweet ass speed trap and racked up tickets for everybody from truckers to little old ladies. Truckers were more difficult because they argued about everything all the time. On the bright side, they never failed to mail in their payments because a suspended license is the last thing a trucker can deal with. Elderly drivers were typically much more pleasant and very rarely argued – easy money.

The only people we hadn't been able to stop yet was a small group of bikers. They always rode in at least a pair, but never more than a trio. They would buzz through town at speeds way above the speed limit, then when they approached our speed trap, they'd engaged the clutch with their left hand and twist the throttle with their right hand, letting their engine revs taunt us as they passed. We'd always give chase, but this is where the strategy in their numbers gave them the advantage. They'd split up, and we've had to choose which one to stick with. Either we'd follow them through town as they blew through stop signs and endangered the residents, or we'd follow them down the highway where their speed would hit triple digits and they'd weave in and out of traffic. Neither one was a good scenario for an officer, as the general rule of thumb is you don't continue with a pursuit if the risk outweighs the reward. Sure, catching these a-holes would be super rewarding for Miller and me, but the risk of serious bodily injury or even death inevitably dictated that we back off every time we had an encounter with them.

These chases would always occur at night, using the veil of darkness to mask details that would be easily spotted in daylight. Color, make, model, license plate numbers, were all more difficult to make out at midnight versus noon. So Miller and I start scheming. We track the frequency of these drive-by's, noting what days they occur on, how many days between each run, time of night, direction of travel, and anything else we can think of. We can also use the darkness to our benefit as well. The only official patrol vehicle we have access to is my pickup, but in the dark, any vehicle can look like a cop car. A quick trip to the nearest music store in Leitchfield provides all the props we need. A revolving light from the stage lighting section plugged into a car's cigarette lighter is more than convincing in the dark as a police signal. We make our best guess as to when the next fly-by will occur and set up a strategic net between the two of us that we can lead them too, minimizing the risk to the locals and maximizing our miniscule resources. If we can funnel them into a trap at the location of our choosing, then we can put an end to this needless risk before somebody gets maimed.

On the first night of our little "stake-out" we end up falling asleep in our cars and not catching shit the whole night. On the second night though, we hit the jackpot. About a quarter til eleven, I hear the whine of a crotch-rocket rapidly approaching. I call Miller over our two-way radios and alert him that it's showtime. I depress the brake pedal and shift my truck from Park to Overdrive in preparation for the impending pursuit. My adrenaline kicks in and time seems to slow down, almost to a stop. My truck isn't the only thing in overdrive as my senses heighten to full alert. In a matter of seconds, the sport bike screams past my usual spot and immediately begins disappearing as the distance between us increases. I slide my foot from the brake pedal and smash it to the floor as soon as I feel the resistance of the gas pedal. Dirt and rocks pelt the undercarriage of my pickup as the tires spin, begging to find purchase in the soil. Now I'm no dummy, I know a pickup truck doesn't stand a chance against a motorcycle that's built for speed, but I don't need to outrun him. I only need to stay in his mirror and try to influence his decisions as he tries to elude me. With any luck I can lead him straight to Miller without him even knowing what's happening. Forget David Copperfield, how's *that* for a magic trick?!

I catch up to him the best I can, hoping to convince him to stick to maneuverability over top speed. If he sticks to the highway, then Miller and I have no chance at busting him. Luckily, I get close enough to make him rethink the raw horsepower option. He lets me gain on him until I'm dangerously close to his rear tire, then suddenly he pulls a Top Gun maneuver. He jams on the brakes, locking up his wheels and making his tires shatter the quiet night air with their screeching. The rider quickly leans to his right, changing the bike's direction onto a side street on the far side of town. He stiffens his right arm to counter-steer and keep the bike upright and avoid laying it down. I admire his skill for the briefest second, then make the next possible right turn on the last road before the town fades into tobacco fields.

I gun the engine trying to make up ground. I look to my right at each intersection hoping to spot my night rider. At the third block, I catch a glimpse of his taillight. He's going considerably slower, most likely thinking that he'd ditched me. At the fourth block, I crank the steering wheel in order to reengage the chase. He must not see me coming because he doesn't react until my truck lurches out right behind him.

He takes off and I give chase, already planning my next moves. I know where this road goes. Evidently, this guy doesn't. In two more blocks, this road makes a forced left turn into a small sub-division and there's only two roads that exit the tiny neighborhood. Miller is sitting at the first one, facing the other in case he needs to shift locations in a hurry. Luckily that's our setup, because the biker foregoes the first option, heading directly for his final turn. I signal Miller over the radio and he adjusts his position accordingly.

The motorcycle quickly approaches the last turn to exit the sub-division and I start to ease off my accelerator. He disappears around the bend, and when I finally ease into the curve I see chaos ensue. Miller's car was still settling into a complete stop with its beacon light burning bright, while the bike was angling in front of the make-shift police cruiser. I see the bike go into another skid, but this one isn't controlled. The rider goes down and kicks his body away from the bike to keep his legs from being pinned underneath the engine and getting burned. The machine slides across the pavement in a shower of sparks. Simultaneously, the human slides across the pavement in a shower of flesh and blood spatter. That can't feel good.

I ease my pickup into a stop and throw the shifter into park. I casually exit my vehicle and stroll over to the downed biker. "Nice night for a ride huh? Sir, do you know why I stopped you tonight?" His response came in the form of a groan. I would have to imagine he's in at least a small amount of pain. I have Miller call for an ambulance while I try to question my perp. "Now I suppose I should go ahead and read you your rights, and just know that somebody will be here shortly to take a look at your wounds." I rattle off his Miranda Rights and immediately follow up with questions. "What the hell are you doing, man? Just looking for a cheap thrill? Trying to antagonize local police and get the thrill of a high-speed chase? Do you have a death wish??"

"It's called recon, numb nuts. You size up your enemy before you attack."

Umm...do what now? "And who exactly are you sizing up?" I inquire.

"You musta misheard me. All I said was I want my attorney." And that comment alone shuts down any further questioning immediately.

Without anything else to discuss, Miller and I have a conversation of our own off to the side, leaving our new friend writhing on the ground in pain. "Did you happen to catch what he said?" I asked Miller. "He's been testing us. He's gotta be with the Bombers."

"No colors," Miller points out.

"Well no shit, detective. If he's gathering intel then he's not gonna broadcast his loyalties and tip his hand. Check his ID. Guarantee it says Owensboro."

Miller steps over to the skinned carcass and pulls his wallet from his back pocket. "Fredericka Street, Owensboro, Kentucky," he confirms. Jackpot. We step back away from ear shot after Miller returns the guy's wallet to his pants pocket.

"You know we're screwed, right?" I ask quietly, to keep our conversation from being overheard.

"How so?"

"As soon as he gets to the hospital and has phone access, he's gonna fill his guys in on everything he knows."

"But what could he possibly know?" Miller asks.

"Quite a lot. He now knows that we have one police cruiser between the two of us along with a rental car that has a stage light in it. I'm sure he's probably already gathered that our police force is comprised solely of us, and it won't be long before they connect the dots and realize that we're both Kings if they don't already know. That alone is a good bit of knowledge about our resources and manpower."

"So what do we do?"

"We cuff his ass and wait for the ambulance. Other than that, not much we can do."

Chapter 17

The next couple days and nights are spent at the clubhouse, planning, anticipating, and strategizing about our next moves as a club. The Bombers are serious and they aren't gonna back off this territory push.

"It's nut up or shut up time," I declare to Scott and Miller who join me at the conference table in our official meeting room. I look Scott directly in the eye, challenging him with my next statement. "You wanted this Prez, are you ready to fight for it?"

"I wasn't interested in all *this*," he confesses. "I wanted to keep the MC alive, but as a legitimate club. I had no intention of continuing the one percenter status. I just wanted to keep the club ingrained in the identity of the town. It's all anybody around here knows and I wanted to keep it that way. I didn't know about all this other behind the scenes shit," he admits.

"How the hell did you think this was gonna turn out?!? You're out here flying outlaw colors in territory known for its drug trade! This is the kind of shit you run into when you rush into things and don't know the history or do the necessary research to see what you're getting yourself into," I lecture him. "Hell, we're basically just pretending to be an MC anyway. Anything less than six members isn't even recognized as a real club. Everybody knows that. And here we are with four."

"This isn't doing us any good right now," Miller finally chimes in. "There's no question Scott is well aware of his mistakes right now. We can't change what's already happened. All we can do is plan for what's coming."

"Or we can stay focused on business," says Jaws, grabbing a seat at the table with the rest of us. Until now, he's been in the corner of the room on his cell phone. The rest of us look at him curiously, anticipating what he has in mind. "My Pop has another batch of shine made up for us, and it's ready for delivery."

I exhale loudly. The thought of making another run to Tennessee and potentially having another interaction with Dirty Mike does not appeal to me the least little bit right now. Who knows, maybe with a little luck we can talk to him about taking some pressure off the Bombers and subsequently, us. Sure, that's likely. "Alright, we'll run it in my truck again. Same approach as before, but this time Jaws and Scott will follow us in his car. I don't want Dirty Mike catching us with our pants down. We need to make sure our heads stay on a swivel and we keep our eyes peeled in every direction. Everybody on the same page?" I look from Scott to Miller to Jaws, and they each begin nodding their head. "Miller and I will go get the truck. You two go get Jaws' car, then we'll meet at the still site. Let's hit it."

We step outside and each of us mount up on our bikes. We fire them up and let the thunder explode from the exhaust pipes. I'm sure the neighbors would hate us if they hadn't already been conditioned to the Kings' shenanigans over the last several decades. One at a time, we pull away from the clubhouse. After a couple turns, Miller and I break off from the other two and drive in the direction of my apartment. Once we park, we head inside for a preemptive bathroom break, because you never know, and while we're at it we decide to leave our vests behind.

In no time we're pulling off the side of the highway and stomping through the weeds back to the little plot where the still is located. Scott and

Jaws pull in right behind us. Miller and I instantly notice that these two idiots are still wearing their vests. "Would you two dumbasses take those off?" Miller asks, leaving no room for negotiating.

"We figured we're handling club business, so we might as well wear our colors," Jaws chimes in.

"Well that's about the dumbest damn logic I've ever heard," Miller retorts. "That's exactly why you *don't* wear your vest, numb nuts. If we get busted bootlegging 'shine while wearing our vests, then the whole club goes down in flames…again. And if you want this club to appear beyond its outlaw past, then the last thing you want to do is get caught doing some outlaw shit while wearing your patch."

"What he said," I confirm. "That's just dumb," I say shaking my head. They both strip their vest and drop them in the trunk of Jaws' car. The more hidden, the better. We load up my pickup with the next load, and it's substantial. I estimate it to be about thirty-five gallons.

"Try forty," Jaws' dad corrects me. "Should be a hefty payday, if you don't screw it up." He seems to have a pretty good intuition about our criminal abilities. "Same setup as before. Same drop point, but be sure to collect the damn money before you bury it with the whiskey. Now my buyer seemed a little off last time I talked to him, so count the cash before you make the drop. Should be ten grand waitin' on you." Not bad!

"What do you mean by your buyer seemed a little off? Like law enforcement might be involved?" I ask.

"Hell no. This guy wouldn't involve the police in nothin'. He just got a little pushier than usual. Tryin' to buy up all my stash."

Hmm. Not sure if that has anything to do with us or if ol' Dirty is just looking to get sloppy drunk on some bathtub liquor. We'll find out soon enough I guess. Jaws and Scott finish loading up the last of the jugs in the back of my truck, then we cover it all with a tarp and throw some other random crap on top for good measure. We go over the strategy for the drop one more time, then hit the road. Miller and I in my truck, Jaws and Scott in the car, just like before.

The hour and a half drive is getting pretty standard at this point, I just have to remember which dead tree the cash is supposed to be in. Jaws and Scott hang back several hundred feet to be our lookout. They appear to have car trouble, and if anybody drives by them then they give a quick honk to let us know that we have company.

We fish the cash out of the hollowed-out tree and start dropping in the booze. The delivery is going smoothly as we get down to the last couple jugs of shine. We haven't heard a peep from our lookout, so we take that as a good sign. Of course, things can't continue to go smoothly, and as Miller and I are hoisting the final two jugs into the hole in the tree a gunshot rings out. Miller instinctively hits the deck and rolls behind a tree, surveying every detail of what's happening. I let a short scream burst from my mouth and cower into a fetal position.

Two more shots chip into the trees near Miller and me. I scurry to find cover behind my truck, then turn to check on Miller. He's oddly calm. I suppose that could be expected given where he's been in the last year.

"They're not trying to hit us," he says. "The shots are ten feet over our heads. Somebody's just screwing with us."

Sure. "Somebody" is trying to screw with us. No telling who that could possibly be. I begin surveying the wooded area and spot a muzzle blast as the next shot rips out. With dusk drawing near its end, the flash of light is easy to spot. It looks to have come from a tree about fifty yards away and twenty feet off the ground. I stand from the cover of my truck and face the direction of the shooter. I don't say anything, but rather stand there, daring him to keep shooting.

"My, how the tables have turned," the comment is yelled from the shooter. No surprise, the voice belongs to Dirty Mike. "Last time we were all together down here and guns were involved, it was my guy that went down. That shit ain't happenin' again!" His tone grows rather outraged by the end.

"Nobody here had anything to do with that. Those guys are all locked up and out of the picture," I point out.

"*You're* here, aren't you dumbass? Or did you forget that you were standing front and center when Jimmy got shot?"

Well, shit. Fair point. "Nobody asked for that to happen. Your boy made a move and got put down. That was his choice and it's on him," I yell back.

"Watch it!" Mike warns. "Choose your next words wisely. It would be smart for you to consider the fact that I don't owe you shit!"

"It would be smart for you to consider the fact that we still serve a purpose," I retaliate. A moment of silence follows, so I assume this is something he hasn't thought about up to this point. "We're bringing you booze, aren't we? Also, how much attention do you think it would draw if you shot a cop??" Still no response. Miller and I pause in silence, waiting to conclude this conversation and go on about our business.

And that's when the silence is shattered by the roar of an engine igniting. Headlights spark to life, and quickly begin bearing down on mine and Miller's location. We spring into the truck and take off as soon as the transmission can find a gear. Hell, at this point, I don't even care if it's the *right* gear…just *a* gear will do; I can shift once we're moving. In the blink of an eye we're approaching Scott and Jaws' location. I flash my lights, honk the horn, crank the siren, and hit the strobes – whatever I can think to get their attention and let them know it's time to go.

I see their headlights turn on and they start to maneuver to U-turn, but they're too slow. Miller and I blaze past them in the truck with Dirty Mike close behind. Once I take a second to examine my rear-view mirror, I instantly recognize the headlights. They are the all-too familiar lamps from a 1973 Mustang that I got uncomfortably close to awhile back on my first trip to this area while I was on my bike, running a backpack for the Kings. At the time, I assumed I was running drugs from Rough River Falls to Tennessee, but as we learned earlier, it turns out I had it backwards.

Our vehicles roar down the back roads, undoubtedly bringing unwanted attention from nosy neighbors who become curious about the noise. I can only imagine how odd the sight has to be, seeing a rusted-out Mustang chasing a police vehicle instead of the other way around. Dirty Mike harasses my rear bumper all the way to the on-ramp for US-24 E. Mustangs aren't really known for their handling abilities, but with Miller and I being in a lifted pickup, we have to take turns even slower with our higher center of gravity. Typically, the 351 cubic-inch V-8 in my truck would be sufficient for most high-speed needs, but not when it's facing off with a 429 Super Cobra Jet. Super. Cobra. Jet. Any of those words by themselves would mean that the vehicle is built for speed, but put them all together and there's no way I stand a chance of outrunning this faded beast.

We have one chance of getting out of this encounter unscathed, and luckily Jaws is on the same page. Him and Scott have beat the Mercury to catch up with the action, and as we all slow down to make the turn onto the on-ramp, Jaws makes contact with the left rear fender of the Mustang, pulling a picture-perfect PIT maneuver and spinning the pony car around one hundred eighty degrees. As the Mustang rolls out of the way I hear Jaws hammer the throttle, and the Mercury speeds up to catch up with me and Miller.

"Hats off to the kid," Miller acknowledges in surprise.

"Agreed," I concur. I wave Jaws around me so he can lead, then I hit the lights and siren to give the appearance of a police escort clear back to Rough River Falls. Holy shit, that was intense. My heart hammers out my pulse quicker than on my prom night, ifyaknowwhatimean. Wink, Wink. Nudge, nudge.

Chapter 18

"Whew, that could've gotten messy," Scott says as we step into the
clubhouse after parking our vehicles in the grass out front and finally donning
our vests.

"Kid, that was quick thinking and even faster driving back there," I
say to Jaws, rounding the corner of the bar and tossing him a bottle of beer. I
start to toss one to Scott, then pull up and throw it in Miller's direction instead.
Scott looks at me incredulously. "You know where they are," I say with a shit-
eating grin on my face.

"As the president of this club, I sure do know where they are," he
retorts, making it a point to mention his position and leaving my position
beneath him unsaid, but implied. I chuckle and nod my head in response,
reaching into the fridge to grab him a chilled bottle. "Here you go, SIR."

We lounge around the clubhouse for the next few hours, blowing off
our adrenaline, cracking jokes at each other's expense, and listening to some
classic rock. But only the hits. Ain't got no time for no deep album cut
bullshit. The essential Lynyrd Skynyrd was up first, because why wouldn't it
be?! Once Kayla's shift at the bar ends, she joins us and relieves me from bar
duty. Before too long, she can't handle the childishness anymore though, so
she gives me a kiss goodbye and heads out to go get some sleep before her
lunch shift later in the morning.

Scott and Jaws recount their story from earlier, what all they heard and
what went through their minds, then I reviewed what Miller and I experienced.
Miller cut in every few sentences to bring my grandiose story-telling back

down to reality, but we eventually got through all of the mindless banter and reliving of what had just played out. As we sit together and laugh at each other's idiocy a brick crashes through the front door window with a note rubber banded around it.

"What the hell?!" I blurt out, flinching at the noise. Scott and Jaws immediately hit the deck. Miller stays as calm as ever. Damn, that dude is a straight-up, cold-blooded badass. I pause for a few seconds to make sure there's nothing else coming our way, then I cautiously stroll over to the brick and read the note out loud, "Mike's done with you. This turf is ours. The Kings are dead." The Kings are dead. I repeat it over in my head.

Scott stands and sticks his face up to the window next to the door. He yells through the panes of glass, "Dead my ass, motherf-" he stops short and retreats from the window. I notice that things get a little brighter for a second before another window crashes from the window frame. A glass jar smashes into the floor, shattering on impact and spraying fire in every direction. Burning liquid from the Molotov cocktail splashes onto Scott and his arm begins to burn. He panics and starts flailing wildly before Miller rushes over to him and begins beating the flame out with his own hands.

"OUT!" I scream. "NOW!" Jaws is already rushing to the door as another fireball sails through the busted window, again spreading fire as far as the liquid inside the jar can spray. There is now a wall of fire dissecting the clubhouse, with Jaws and me on one side and Scott and Miller on the other. "LET'S GO!" I bark through the fire. Jaws is now standing in the open door frame, looking back into the clubhouse to make sure we're all coming. I scurry closer to his location while also making sure that Miller and Scott are following.

Another bottle flies in, showering more of the clubhouse in flames. Miller jumps through the fire, landing directly in front of me. I see Scott preparing to make his jump as the next fire bomb passes through the window. This time though, instead of crashing down on the floor and further igniting, I hear a very distinct thud. I see it impact Scott's skull, then fall to the ground without breaking. The liquid inside pours out, creating a concentrated area of intense heat. Simultaneously, Scott's body falls to the floor with the bottle. I start to react to grab Scott and pull him out of the fire, but there's too much. The flames have engulfed the clubhouse and I can barely make out Scott's torso. The smoke is starting to bellow as the flames devour the furniture and everything inside. The air is toxic from the smoke and the temperature is unbearable.

It's now or never. And never isn't an option. I pull my vest over my head and leap into the fire, hoping that there's a clear landing spot on the other side. As soon as my feet hit the floor, I bend down, grab his arm, and start pulling. He's unresponsive and limp. There's no good or easy way to get through this, so I just try to move as quickly as possible without stopping. I yank his body through the inferno until I reach Miller on the other side. He picks up Scott's legs and we carry him outside, dangling between the two of us like a lifeless human hammock. His jeans are still burning, so we roll him over to suffocate the flame.

Jaws is already calling the small, volunteer fire department that resides across town. Similar to the newly formed police force, the Rough River Falls Fire Department consists of a small, but well-kept fire house along with a couple firetrucks. The town provided the building, vehicles, and equipment, but had no budget to pay the firefighters so they rely solely on volunteers. While that's happening, I sprint to my truck and grab my police radio, requesting support from any Grayson County Sheriff's deputies that might happen to be in the not-too-distant area. During this chaos, I can't help but notice a group of bikers speeding away from the property. Not that I needed any further confirmation, but this left no doubt that the Bombers were behind this attack.

Being trained first responders, Miller and I do our best to work on Scott until backup arrives. There's no time to wait for an ambulance to be dispatched, drive to Rough River Falls to get him, then return back to the hospital before he can be checked out, so I make a call. "Get him in the truck," I order. Miller and Jaws carefully load him into the bed of my pickup. This is certainly not the type of medical care anybody should ever receive, but this is what we've got so this is what we're going with. I jump into the driver's seat. Miller slides into the passenger seat, and Jaws pops a squat in the back with Scott. "Hang on!" I yell to Jaws through my window as I flip the lights and siren and mash the gas pedal. I jerk the wheel and spin my truck around to face the opposite direction. We blow through town and beat hell trying to get to Grayson County Medical Center.

We come to a screeching halt in the emergency bay. Nurses and a triage doctor meet us at the door with a gurney. We transfer Scott as quickly and carefully as possible from the back of my pickup to the bed before they wheel him inside.

"What's the story?" asks the doctor.

"He got caught in a fire. Bad burns on his arm and legs minimum. He was unconscious when we pulled him out and he hasn't come to since then," I reply.

"We'll take it from here," she acknowledges. As they rush deeper into the building I hear the doctor handing out orders. "Get his clothes cut off and get him oxygen now," she instructs calmly. There's a good chance she's the only one that's calm right now...

Chapter 19

"Listen, Kayla, just get to the Grayson County Med Center and I'll explain everything," I plead with her, my call waking her from her slumber.

"I'm on my way," she concedes. I know she wants to know what's going on, but this isn't really the type of story you tell somebody over the phone. Plus, she's gonna want to be here with Scott.

Miller, Jaws, and I go ahead and get examined by an ER doc to make sure none of us took in too much smoke or were burned without realizing. That last part might sound ridiculous, but with the adrenaline and all our attention being on Scott, it would be nothing to ignore a minor injury. The mind is a powerful thing. We each get checked out and return to the waiting area without any updates on Scott's condition.

Kayla scurries in and immediately wants the complete run down of events after she left the clubhouse. I explain the brick, our uninvited guests, and the firebombing they brought with them. I try to spare her the graphic details, but she clearly wants the full story. I do my best to give that to her, while still trying to tap dance around the specifics of the unforgettable smell of burning flesh and human hair. She does her best to keep her composure, but I can read her thoughts like a book. She's a complete wreck inside, worrying about Scott. After their parents died in a tragic accident, Kayla finished raising Scott and he is the only family she has left.

We grab small paper cups of the worst coffee I've ever had in my life, just so we have something to do while we wait. We sit in silence, the emotional distress clearly weighing on all of us in our own ways. Miller even appears to be shaken up, which kind of surprises me. I've seen him keep his cool literally under fire and on top of that, he barely knows the kid. I can only imagine he's realizing how real things just got for the club, and how wildly unprepared we were for something of this magnitude.

We finally see the doctor appear through the automatic doors that lead to the operating rooms. She has a grim look on her face as she approaches our group. Background noise disappears and her speech comes out in muted, barely audible tones. It's like a scene from a cheesy movie or poorly written novel. "There's no easy way to say this. We cleaned his wounds to get a compete assessment of the injuries. Your friend-"

"Brother," we all correct in unison.

"Your brother," she revises, "suffered second and third degree burns over a lot of his arms, torso, and legs. There was also a great deal of smoke inhalation in addition to the head trauma. From what I can tell, the blow to the head knocked him out. The massive amount of shock that his body and brain went through kept him from waking up. I'm sorry. We did everything we could."

Kayla melts to the floor instantly, devastated from what we've just heard. I squat down to embrace her and she leans into me, knocking me onto my butt. "I don't know what to do," she says, weeping. I can feel the sense of utter loss in her words. I hold onto her for several minutes on the floor, before trying to stand us both up.

"Screw you!" comes her reaction. It catches me completely off guard, and I don't know how to respond. I can't even comprehend if that's what she actually said. I try to guide her back to a chair when she says it again. "Screw you!" More forceful this time. "How did you let this happen?? You know he's the only family I have left! You were supposed to keep him safe…protect him from this shit!"

I don't know how to respond, so I just stand there for a moment, soaking it in. "Kayla, I'm sorry," I eventually mutter.

"Oh, you're sorry? *YOU'RE* sorry?!? That's not gonna bring my brother back!" she seethes.

"This was *HIS* idea!" I point out. Sure, get defensive and blame the dead guy. That's definitely the best approach in this situation. The one thing people who are grieving really love is hearing how their loved one was ultimately responsible for their own demise. I immediately realize my mistake when I see my words smack Kayla across her face. She physically recoils and pulls herself further away from me.

"You should go," she mutters.

I open my mouth to try to take back the interaction, but nothing comes out. I can only look at her, silently pleading with my eyes for her to understand this wasn't my doing. I get the clear sense that she is completely disgusted by me, so I turn to walk away. "Come on guys, we need to figure out what's going on," I say to Miller and Jaws who quietly join behind me.

*****

We drive back to Rough River Falls in silence. None of us knowing what to say or even how to process the events that have just occurred. I pull into the small, makeshift police headquarters/jail without even thinking about it. I just know we need someplace to decompress and debrief, and our normal place isn't much of a place anymore. Not to mention it's a crime scene.

"Miller, we need to start writing official narratives on this while it's still fresh. Jaws, gonna need your account of what you experienced too." This isn't something that we can sweep under the rug and handle in the standard operating procedure of typical outlaw motorcycle clubs. I wouldn't have been able to do that when the Kings were legitimate outlaws, even more so now that the club was trying to take a different path. I'm no longer undercover, so the ruse of being part of that world is gone completely. This has to be handled in an official capacity with a complete investigation…even if there's no question who perpetrated the incident.

We spend hours at the station, bouncing from one menial task to the next. We write up our personal accounts, make meaningless small talk, and try to formulate a plan of how to proceed with our investigation.

The first thing I do is call the Owensboro Police Department. I identify myself and give a brief rundown of the events from the night. I ask if they have any open cases against the Bombers. The Shift Sergeant mentions some of the typical stuff like noise complaints around the clubhouse, maintaining a common nuisance charge for some of their parties, but nothing ever more serious than a small fine and a slap on the wrist. He suggests that I contact the Kentucky State Police to see if maybe they have anything more substantial to share.

I thank him for his help and take his tip. KSP either didn't have anything to share, or didn't feel it necessary to share info if they *did* have anything on the Bombers, but making this call gives me the best idea I could come up with. As soon as I hang up with the very unhelpful Post Commander,

I start scrolling through my contacts. I find what I was looking for and hit the green send button. In no time, I'm talking to my former DEA contact.

"Well if it isn't Ponch himself," he begins, answering my call. Enough with the cheesy references already.

I cut him off, not in the mood for sarcastic pleasantries. Damn, re-read that sentence. If that isn't an indicator that this shit is deep then I don't know what is! I try not to be rude, but make it quite apparent that this is a business call. "Listen man, I need some intel." I give him the rundown and he exhales with a long, slow breath.

"Will, what have you gotten yourself into?"

"That's what I'm trying to figure out. My initial investigation into the Kings had it wrong. They're all still guilty as shit, but my accusations were backwards. They weren't the source of the drugs, they were the distributors. Evidently, the Bluegrass Bombers are another distributor, and I set off a chain reaction when I made my bust."

"Well, yeah, we got all that figured out a while ago. You were onto something, which is why those guys are still behind bars, but we managed to put some more pieces of the puzzle together after your departure. The drugs are coming from a trailer park in Tennessee, and there's an entire network of MC's that are distributing throughout Kentucky like the Kings were. Obviously, the Bombers are part of that network, and they've absorbed a lot of the impact of the Kings' absence because of their location in the city. You've made some bad enemies, as you have quickly found out. You need to figure out an end game and shut this shit down before anybody else gets hurt, Will. We aren't talking about the Kings of Chaos anymore. Those guys were a bunch of hoodlums without anybody looking over their shoulder. The Bombers have a *lot* of people looking over their shoulder, but they still manage to operate. They figure out ways to get things done while living under a microscope. I don't need to tell you that's a lot scarier than a group of guys ruling a hilljack town in the country."

As a native of that hilljack country town, I bristle at his analysis of my village but I can't argue his point regardless. "Do you guys have anything on them? Can you throw me a bone? I'm not asking for your entire file. I'm asking for a breadcrumb to throw at them and try to slow them down a little bit. Buy me some time to get shit figured out."

"You already have what you need, Will," he points out. "You're an officer of the law. You witnessed their guys leaving the scene earlier. If you can identify a single one of them then you're in business. Even if you can't, you still know their business and where their source of product comes from. Throw some weight around. Keep an eye on them. That should give you a little breathing room to plan your next steps. If it helps, we've got you covered with your matters in Tennessee. He's got some federal charges coming his way with his enterprise crossing state lines. But do yourself a favor and stay away from that area. I don't know what kind of arrangements you have down there, but you really don't need to be putting yourself on anybody's radar."

"Got it. Don't worry, I have no reason to go back. Thanks for the advice." Dammit, I'm really bad at what I do. He's right about all of that of course. That's the thing about those DEA guys. They're pretty damn smart. I don't have to tip toe through the shadows anymore. Everybody knows my official role in the community. I'm not undercover, so I don't have to pretend to be an outlaw while trying not to slip too far down that rabbit hole. I have nothing to hide anymore – well, at least nothing to hide since the Kings bust. Welp enough reminiscing. Time to make some noise.

Chapter 20

The sun has already risen before we finally decide to leave the station and start making our next moves. I dismiss Jaws, telling him to go home and hang up his colors. He stares at me in disbelief, showing every emotion imaginable in a single look. I already know exactly what he's thinking, so I speak up. "It's over, Jaws. We tried to keep this club around and for what? What was the point? To save the town? To give Scott something to do? Well it didn't work. We weren't ready for this shit and we got Scott killed. This club is dead too. The Kings no longer serve a purpose in this community. These colors don't offer the same kind of protection that they used to. In fact, they do quite the opposite. We brought harm to this town *because* of these colors! The new Kings were a sham of a club. The presence of the patch doesn't restore or normalize the gaping absence from the town. Only me, serving in my official capacity, has had any kind of influence that would reminisce of the order that the real club provided to Rough River Falls. And I've worked my ass off to get things back in line around here. Just go home, Jaws. It's over. Now it's time for me and Miller to take over."

"What the hell am I supposed to do?" he asks. His voice is quiet and uncertain, betraying the brother that we've come to know who'll stand toe-to-toe with anybody when excrement hits a spinning rotor.

"Go check on your dad. Take over the club's portion of the partnership with your old man. Run 'shine and make money. You don't have to worry about getting busted around here as long as I'm around, but let your dad know that his Tennessee customer is out of the picture."

Jaws stands there for a minute. Not in defiance or disbelief, but rather just letting it all sink in I think. He looks back and forth between me and Miller a couple times. Without saying anything, Miller and I slide our vests off and hang them on the backs of our desk chairs, then grab our shields and sidearms; literally dropping our patches for our badges before Jaws finally turns to leave.

"Miller, we need to change, but no uniforms," I say to him as we follow Jaws outside. He nods in acknowledgement. Nothing else is said during the drive back to my apartment.

We each clean ourselves up and grab some clean clothes – plain clothes. Like I mentioned, no uniforms yet. We need to kick this investigation into overdrive, but we need to create a little space between us and the Bombers so we can breathe and figure out where we go from here. Miller is already on the same page as me. There's a weird bond between partners. You get used to each other's thought processes and learn how to predict their tendencies. He already knows my plan without me saying a word about it.

We're going to take a nice drive up to Owensboro in my pickup truck. You know, the one that has the police markings on it? The weather is pretty much perfect, so it'll be a great day to soak up some sun and just hang out in a quiet neighborhood. I think there's a park that just happens to be across the street from the Bombers clubhouse. Coincidentally, I think that might be my favorite place to go and do some people watching. Since we'll be well outside our jurisdiction we won't be in uniform and we won't be serving in any official capacity. Just a couple guys enjoying some fresh air. How am I supposed to know if our presence will give the Bombers a certain type of impression? I have no control over their paranoia and if they feel that they're being watched by law enforcement. Maybe don't be a criminal, then you wouldn't have to worry.

We take Highway 54 all the way from Rough River Falls straight into Owensboro. We know we're getting close to the city when we hear the roar of race car engines getting in some practice laps at Kentucky Motor Speedway. The track lays just outside of a speck on the map called Philpot, right before Highway 54 turns into Leitchfield Road. We come to US-60 on the eastside of Owensboro and Leitchfield Road splits off and becomes Parrish Avenue. A few blocks later we arrive at Chautauqua Park. The park is flanked on the west and north sides by some commercial businesses and warehouse type buildings. The south and east sides of the park butt right up to a run-down little neighborhood, with modest homes in some type of disrepair and decade old vehicles lining driveways and street parking.

We spot the Bomber's clubhouse clearly marked at the corner of Alexander Avenue and 15th Street. Typically, when you are surveilling a residence you stop before you get to it, that way you don't rouse suspicion from anybody inside as you drive by. However, that's exactly what we wanted to do, so we drove directly in front of the clubhouse, nice and slow, until we reached the southwest corner of the park. As I parked on a grassy patch next to a baseball field, I turned my truck so the police markings would be as visible as possible from the clubhouse.

Once the truck was in park and I killed the engine, Miller and I hopped down from the seats and strolled to the rear tailgate. We popped a squat on the back of the truck after lowering the tailgate, and began eating the burgers we had grabbed at a drive-thru on the way into town. It would've been a lot easier to garner attention if Miller and I had been in a more jovial, raucous mood. Unfortunately, given the recent events, neither of us was feeling too talkative. So, once we finished our early lunch, I did the next best thing.

Crumpling up my sandwich wrapper and tossing it back in the bag (don't litter folks, that's bad), I casually walked back around to the driver's door. Wrapping my hand around the handle, I gave it a yank and slowly opened the door. From outside the truck, I reached in and gave the horn a long, loud blast. I like to think the honk sounded angry because that's how I feel, but that's probably projecting a little too much. After that, I close the door and wander back to the bed of my pickup, returning to my seat next to Miller, and wait.

It's not long before Miller elbows me to get my attention. He's sitting on the side closest to the clubhouse and I had let my gaze wander off into the park in the opposite direction. I turn my head and immediately spot why Miller was nudging me. Bruiser, The Bombers Prez, is pounding the pavement to beat the band in our direction. The look on his face seems casual, but his brisk pace implies a different emotion completely.

"What?" comes his opening line as he approaches our parking spot. Well said. Very eloquent. I can tell he's not amused by our presence, but I'm in no frame of mind to give two shits.

"Shut up," I instruct. "I'm in no mood to play around with you."

"You may have forgotten where you are," he replies. "Last time you told me to jump and flashed a badge, expectin' me to do exactly what you said. That may have worked when we were in your hick town where your authority reigns, but yer outside yer jurisdiction now, so I don't know where you get off thinkin' that yer gonna tell me what to do."

"Maybe you missed the part where I'm not here to play games," I begin.

He cuts me off. "Good, cuz neither am I."

I look at him, my mouth still open from not getting to finish my thought. My gaze bores straight through him and I deliberately close my mouth, urging him to continue. Let's see where this goes.

"From what I'm hearin' on the news, it sounds like our expansion may come sooner than later," he says, referring to the Bombers taking over the Kings' territory. "Hell, probably won't even need to patch you over at this point," he taunts.

I slide down from the tailgate of my truck where I was perched and say my next sentence slowly, so there's no confusion. "Choose your next words wisely, because one more crack like that and you'll never have to worry about territory again." It comes out of my mouth in barely over a whisper, but certainly loud enough to be heard by all three of us. The chill of my voice is unsettling even to me. Talk about an effective threat! "I want a meeting. A week from today. Let's go with noon." I stick my thumb toward Miller, gesturing between the two of us. "We have to make arrangements to bury a brother first, then get him laid to rest," I switch the motion from Miller to Bruiser, exchanging my thumb for my index finger. "After that, we have business that needs handled," motioning between Bruiser and myself now. We certainly have business, and it will be handled on my terms. In my town.

He nods, weighing my request. "We'll be there alright," he agrees.

"But you better be ready to tell us what we want to hear. Wouldn't want another unfortunate accident to happen to you guys."

He barely gets his sentence finished before Miller rises from his seat on my tailgate, standing immediately to Bruiser's right. The movement catches Bruiser's attention, so he turns his head toward Miller. As his head rotates to his right, Miller throws a massive left hook. The momentum of his fist and Bruiser's head moving in opposite directions amplifies the impact. Normally, if you're gonna take a punch, you want to move with it, so the strike glances off, causing minimal damage. The exact opposite happened in this instance, and I see Bruiser's eyes roll immediately back into his skull. His knees turn to rubber and he wobbles forward a couple steps before his legs completely give out and he crumples to the ground, unconscious. Holy shit, that was a shot even I didn't see coming!

"Welp, looks like we're done here then," I say to Miller. "Let's get going before anybody else wanders over from the clubhouse. This isn't the time or place to get rat packed by a bunch of pissed off outlaws." Miller has no reaction, but we return to our seats in the truck.

I hit the ignition and we make our way back out of town. We got what we came for. The Bombers know we're watching, and I just bought us a week to get things settled in Rough River Falls.

Now to come up with a plan.

Chapter 21

I drop Miller off at my apartment, then head over to Rusty's Tavern. I stick my head inside the dining room area briefly to see if Kayla is working. I don't expect her to be, but I also know that a lot of people need the distraction to keep their mind busy while they cope with the loss of a loved one, to keep them from completely falling apart. When I don't see her hustling through the maze of tables, I glance over to the bar to see if I spot her over there. Still, no sign of her at work. I duck out of the entrance and walk to the side of the business, where the stairwell leads up to Kayla's modest one-bedroom apartment.

I knock three times once I reach the landing at the top of the stairs. "It's open," comes the response from inside. That's probably not safe.

"Might not wanna leave your door open like that," I offer as I step inside.

"Who cares?" is her response. I have no rebuttal for that. How do you argue against that kind of approach?

She looks like hell. She's curled up in one corner of her couch, draped in a blanket. There are brochures and sales flyers scattered around her for caskets, burial plots, headstones and funeral home services. Her eyes are red and puffy, obviously a direct result of nonstop crying. Any remaining makeup she's wearing has already run down her face in streaks. The puffy redness is surrounded by dark circles from a lack of sleep. Her cheeks are flush and void of color.

I take a seat on the couch next to her. I reach over and pull her into me. She doesn't resist, and after a few seconds I feel her shoulders rising and falling as she sobs into my shoulder. My heart breaks, having no idea what she's going through. I've lost family members, but my family had a different dynamic than what Kayla and Scott had. They had been through so much together and were left with only each other. Now that had been ripped from Kayla and I don't know how she's going to get through this.

We sit in silence for what seems like eternity, before I finally find my voice. "I'm sorry," I say. My voice meek and cracking through emotion.

"I know," she acknowledges.

"How can I help?"

"I don't even know where to start," she responds. "I've done this before, but it's different this time. After their accident, I had to make arrangements for my parents by myself. Scott was still too young to help with those plans. I did it then for him. I took that on myself to save him from having to think about it. Everything I've ever done has been for him."

Her entire adult life has been motivated by caring for her brother. She started working at the tavern so she could support him. She lived in this shitty apartment so they'd both have a place to stay together. Sure, she could've left town and moved to the city at some point to have a better life, but ultimately, she was afraid Scott would end up like Brad Olsen. The only difference is that Scott's dad wasn't a state representative, so it wouldn't have even been a blip on the radar.

"It's different this time," she continues. I don't have that factor now. I don't even know what clothes to dress him in. All he ever wore was that damn vest."

"Well there you go then. I think that's your answer."

"I'm not doin' that," she defies. "That patch is what got him killed. I'm not laying him into the ground with that effing reminder!"

"He would've wanted it, Kayla. If you really think about it, I think you know that. You said it yourself. The Kings were the only constant in his life other than you."

"If this is your way of helping, then you can stop."

We continue back and forth for another couple minutes, but I shut it down knowing that I'm not getting anywhere. This isn't something she's gonna back down on. I finally suggest a pair of jeans and a button down plaid shirt. Hard to go wrong with that. Once we settle on the clothes, we methodically move through the plans, one thing at a time.

Without realizing it, the sun has set and darkness has fallen. We both nod off on her couch, sleeping for who knows how long. My stomach wakes me, turning and rumbling, begging for food. I offer to run down to the tavern and grab a bite, but her appetite still hasn't returned.

"I think I'm just ready for some rest," she says. I take the hint and begin walking toward the door.

"Hey," I say, getting her attention. "We made it through the first day. That's a start." She makes some subtle facial expressions, but nothing I can classify as a full gesture; she almost purses her lips, almost tips her head, and almost smiles subtly at the realization. Without showing any emotion completely, she stands and walks back toward her bedroom. "I'll lock your door behind me," I call after her.

I walk down to the bar and order a couple burgers and fries to go. I grab a beer while I'm waiting on the food. Once the order is up, I finally make my way back to my apartment.

Miller is kicked back in the recliner watching some pointless show about driving semi-trucks on ice when I walk in the front door. "Dude, I'm hungry," he says.

I pass him the bag of food before grabbing a couple beers from the fridge. "How's the hand, champ?" I inquire, surprised he doesn't have some ice on it after the haymaker he delivered earlier today.

He waves off my question. "I'm sure it'll be a little sore for the next few days. Wanna grab some ketchup while you're in there?"

We eat in silence. Vegging out on the mindless drivel that's in mid-marathon on the ol' boob tube. Once the food is gone, my mind has been numbed enough. I decide to call it a day.

*****

The morning rolls in and the sun breaks through the cracks in my window blinds. I roll out of bed and grab a pair of jeans and a wrinkled-up t-shirt. I stumble into the living room and find Miller out cold, still occupying the recliner. Several empty bottles line the bottom edge of the chair on the floor. He groans when I enter the room.

"G'morning," I say.

"Stop yelling," he responds, grabbing his head. I know exactly what he needs.

I walk to the kitchen and grab a pitcher from a cabinet above the fridge. I fill it with water and take it to him.

"What's this?" he asks. "No cup?"

"It's my hangover remedy. No cup. Drink up," I instruct. He abides. "I need to run an errand. Keep drinking that water and get rehydrated. I'll be back soon." He nods while raising the pitcher to his mouth. I slide my boots on before walking outside.

I step out into the blinding sunlight. It takes a moment before my eyes adjust to the brightness. As I turn to close the door, I can't help but notice that my neighbor's front door is open, leaving just the storm door between her living room and the great outdoors. I can see the filth from where I'm standing. A few short months ago, I took exception to this lady and her parenting abilities. I had seen her sleeping on the couch with a lit cigarette dangling from her mouth while her toddler roamed around the apartment in nothing but a diaper. She had shacked up with one of the low-life members of the former Kings, Stitch, who she fought with constantly. I know what it felt like to be that kid, because when I was younger, I *was* that kid. Just substitute the mother for my father and it's essentially the same scenario.

Seeing things from this angle though changed my perception a little bit. Stitch was locked up and likely wouldn't be getting out anytime soon. Her son had been stripped from her custody, presumably because of her phenomenal parenting skills. It appears that she had just given up, since everything else had been taken from her. Her apartment mirrored mine when it had been broken into and ransacked prior to my return. Except I don't think anybody would have any interest in rummaging through that dumpster of an apartment.

I just shake my head in disgust and start walking toward the parking area in front of my apartment complex. Maybe pity would be a more accurate description of what I was feeling toward her currently. I get to my spot and throw my leg over the saddle on my Victory. I can use some space and time to clear my mind, and there's no better way to do that than on my bike.

I fire up the engine and the exhaust note rings out. What a beautiful, calming noise. I can feel the tension in my muscles begin to melt away already. I walk the bike backward, out of the parking space and point it in the direction of the street that runs in front of my building. I squeeze my left hand, engaging the clutch and kick my left leg down on the shifter, dropping it into first gear. I slowly release my grip on the clutch and begin to roll on the throttle in my right hand, my bike accelerating underneath me as I do.

I make a couple quick turns and find myself riding down Main Street, passing by Rusty's before approaching the Gas N' Go. I survey the traffic and make a U-turn in front of the town's gas station, parking directly in front of my own personal police station.

I stroll inside and grab a clear property bag off the corner of my desk. I go straight back to my bike and stash it in the saddlebag on the opposite side of my bike than the exhaust pipes. I mount back up, stand the bike up, and swing the kickstand toward the frame. "Let's go for one last ride," I say to myself.

A couple blocks from Main Street I find myself parking in front of the local funeral home. I grab the package from my saddle bag, and walk around the side of the building toward the back entrance. I knock on the door and in no time, it swings open. The funeral director greets me on the other side.

"Hey Mark," I greet him. I look around him and see a body on the slab behind him in the embalming room. My heart sinks to my stomach.

"Will, how are you?" he asks.

"Been better. Listen, I have a request." I dispatch the notion of small talk.

"Sure, come on in," he invites, stepping aside so I can get by him. "What can I do for you?"

"You're gonna be meeting with Kayla today, right? So she can leave instructions on his appearance?" He nods. "I want this in the casket with him." I pull Scott's vest out of the property bag and hand it over to Mark. I can sense his hesitation. "Just wrap it around his legs, in the lower part of the casket where you can't see anything. I don't want him to wear it. Kayla would never go for that and it would destroy her if she sees it in there, but I know Scott would be pissed if he doesn't have it." I feel him starting to come around. "Mark, this is something between Scott and I. I'm not asking for anything crazy here. Just make sure this is in there with him. But do me a favor and keep it out of sight." He nods again.

"Sure thing, Will. I'll do what I can."

With that, I depart from town on my bike. I ride toward the Highway 54-110 split, leaning my bike to the right and driving directly to Rough River Falls State Park. I slow down to a snail's pace, dropping the Kingpin down into first, ride up the steep entryway and find myself alone at the top of the overlook. I leave my bike in the parking lot and walk toward the picnic area, grabbing a bench and dragging it toward the fencing at the edge of the overlook. I fall back onto the bench and bury my head into my hands. With no one around, I finally allow myself to break down. The reality of the last two days crashing into me like a wrecking ball.

Chapter 22

The next couple days I try to spend as much time as possible with Kayla to make sure she knows that she isn't going through this alone. I can feel her withdrawing every time I walk into her apartment, try to give her a hug, or offer to get her some food.

Her coldness toward me can only be attributed to the part she thinks I played in Scott's death by participating in his hairbrained idea to keep the club going. I'm well aware that she just wants me to go away and leave her alone, but there's no chance that's gonna happen right now. The last thing I'm gonna do is abandon her while she's dealing with all this, whether she wants me to or not. I'm not a complete idiot though, so I try to make sure I give her some space and solitude to cope with her emotions when she needs it.

The night before Scott's funeral is the toughest. She wants no part of me and insists on telling me that. Repeatedly. After awhile, I can't help but start to take it personally. She ends up closing herself in her bedroom after a rather heated exchange and proceeds to give me the silent treatment for the rest of the night. I crash on her couch, just to be near in case she has a change of heart.

Part way through the night, I awake to the sound of retching coming from the bathroom across from her bedroom. I shake off the grogginess and get up as quickly as I can, considering I'm coming to from a deep sleep, making my way down the short hallway to Kayla's location. I expect to find her hunched over the toilet, her emotions manifesting physically from her stomach.

Au contraire! She is balled up on the floor, vomit smeared across the linoleum covered floor. She's shaking violently with froth coming from her mouth. As the scene is assaulting my senses I notice an open medicine bottle on the floor next to her. "Kayla!" I scream. No response. I immediately call for an ambulance and advise the dispatcher of the situation.

"Early thirties female, slender frame, apparent overdose. Non-responsive. Spilled bottle of expired hydrocodone was found by her body when she was discovered. She's currently in a rescue position on her side so she doesn't choke on her own vomit. Her head is positioned on top of her arm to keep her airway as open as possible. Please just hurry," I plead. The dispatcher on the other end is trained well and keeps an even, calm tone throughout the call.

Just because the FDA makes pharmaceutical companies put expiration dates on medication doesn't mean that they stop being effective once they pass their prime. Enough of anything can be bad news; prescription narcotics even more so.

The best thing about this scene is the barf sprayed across the floor. That's the best sign I've seen so far, indicating that Kayla's body is trying to save itself. I continually check her pulse and breathing, to ensure the drugs that have already invaded her bloodstream don't begin to shut down her respiratory or cardiovascular systems. Her skin is already clammy. Her breathing is shallow and rapid, with a slow, erratic pulse.

For the next nine minutes I freak the eff out, knowing there's not a damn thing I can do until the paramedics arrive. The only positive I can find solace in is that there are still signs of life. I hear the knock on the door and sprint to open it. They rush in as I yell behind them where to find her. They check her vitals as I give them the same rundown I gave to the dispatcher. They're already well aware of the situation, of course, but I don't know what else to do or say to try to help. This feeling of helplessness is overwhelming, especially as a certified first responder.

The EMT's kneel down in the puddle of puke, roll her onto her back and administer a dose of Narloxone spray into her nostrils. It's more commonly known as Narcan, but even more importantly, it's known for reviving opiate overdose patients. One of the medics briskly exits the small bathroom and goes back outside, returning a moment later with a stretcher, after making a racket trying to get it up the stairs. The two EMT's are able to slow down and further assess the situation now that the Narcan is beginning to counteract the effects of the pills that Kayla ate.

I provide more information about what she's been going through and mention that she hasn't eaten much the past few days. This is an important detail that I spaced out until right now. Because she hadn't been eating much, her stomach was empty and there was nothing in there to soak up any of the medication, leaving a more potent dosage to gain access to her bloodstream. After hearing this, the paramedics begin pumping her full of charcoal as soon as they reach the ambulance outside. Charcoal is a time-tested remedy for overdoses as it has unparalleled absorbing qualities. The biggest side effect is it makes your poop black.

I jump in the back of the ambulance as they close the doors and prepare to transport Kayla to Grayson County Medical Center. The ride goes quickly, but isn't as frantic as I would expect. I assume it helps that they already know the situation and are on top of it. When we arrive, she's whisked away to a curtained off corner of the Emergency Room, and I'm left standing in the all-too-familiar waiting room.

Morning comes before I get an update on Kayla. The ER doctor greets me and gives me the rundown. They had to pump her stomach to cleanse it from all of the pills she had swallowed. They managed to get her stable, but she's still in bad shape.

"Can I see her now?" I ask.

"She had one request when she regained consciousness. Sorry, but she doesn't want any visitors." There's no doubt the doctor sees the dejection in my reaction to her words. "Don't worry. She's safe here. We'll keep a close eye on her and make sure she gets the help she needs."

"How long do you plan on keeping her? Her brother's funeral is today."

"Well, I can't discuss specific treatment plans. What I can tell you is that typically, overdose patients are required to complete a psych eval prior to being discharged. That only happens once we're confident their system has been flushed completely of any foreign chemicals. That whole process could take anywhere from two to three days on the short end or somewhere closer to two weeks depending on how full our psychologist's calendar is, what type of drug was used for the overdose, if the patient has any history of drug use that would build up a tolerance, and the actual result of the evaluation. Medically speaking, I don't see any way she will be released soon enough to attend her brother's funeral today."

I don't even know how to react. I can't imagine how she'll react to missing his services.

The doctor continues. "Having said all that, she is an adult and is able to check herself out anytime she pleases. We can't legally hold her against her will unless a power of attorney exists that can step forward and have her committed."

That last statement almost sounded like a hopeful question, but I shake my head knowing that person doesn't exist. "Take good care of her, doc," I say before spinning on my heels and walking toward the exit.

My mind is numb. I have to attend my club president's funeral in a few short hours, and my old lady just tried to make a sudden exit from the earth in an attempt to reunite her family. With my thoughts racing, I slowly pull my phone from my pocket and call Miller to come pick me up.

Chapter 23

The morning drags by. I take my time shaving, showering, and getting dressed, yet somehow I'm done with all that in less than forty-five minutes. That leaves me with about three hours to sit around and waste time until the viewing hours start at the funeral home. The clock taunts me every second, defying all concept of time throughout the morning.

I make sure to be the first person at the funeral home. Since Kayla is otherwise preoccupied, it only makes sense that I step in and represent Scott like any real brother would. Miller rides with me, providing the same sentiment. Jaws pulls into a parking spot next to us as we're walking in.

The three of us meet in front of the casket and share a hug. None of us knows what to say, so we don't say anything. Normally, this would be my sarcastic ass's time to shine but I just don't have it in me right now. I just feel emotionally exhausted; drained of all feelings. It's called Emotional Fatigue, or EF for short. It's when you share traumatic experiences with those around you, either directly by living through it with the person or indirectly by experiencing their account of it afterward. And it's different than ED. Yep, there it is. I guess I haven't totally lost it.

The next two hours are shared by the three of us greeting anybody who shows up, which isn't that many. Scott's reputation wasn't that great around town. Random teachers from his school days showed up, which was a crazy blast from the past. Scott was a couple years younger than Kayla and I, but we all still had the same teachers pretty much. My reputation with them wasn't all that great either, but in their eyes, I had at least proved my worth by going off and joining the military. Scott just got high and passed out on sidewalks around town, rightfully earning his road name with the Kings. His teachers wrote him off when he was still in school, after his parents died, and he picked up his addiction. They quickly abandoned any idea of trying to work with him and help keep him on the right path.

Of course, this isn't the time or place to bring that topic up, so I shake hands, return half-hearted smiles, and give the occasional hug to people who feel the need to comfort Scott's survivors. I appreciate the gesture of them showing up at least, even if everybody knows they aren't here out of any kind of deep empathy. In a small community, you just show up at the funeral home whenever there's a funeral. It's the polite thing to do.

Finally, the funeral director indicates it's time to share a few words regarding the deceased. Nobody has prepared anything, because we weren't really expecting to be the face of the day, so he spouts some generic drivel that's supposed to be inspiring and uplifting. Sure man. Whatever you say.

At the end of the service, the funeral director releases everyone with a prayer, then Miller, me, and Jaws help him wheel the casket outside to the hearse, where the four of us slide it onto the rollers in the back of the vehicle and secure it in place for the three-block trip to the cemetery. We all follow behind in our own vehicles, the magnetic purple funeral procession flags whipping in the wind from the hoods of our cars. Once we arrive, it's up to the four of us to roll the casket back out, and deliver it onto the cradle to be lowered into the ground.

The funeral director begins to address us again with his interchangeable monologue, but I ask him not to. At the same time, Jaws has walked back to his car and returned with something in his hand. He approaches the casket and splays out his Kings of Chaos vest right on top of the casket. Kayla isn't here to object, and the gesture catches me completely off guard. My throat sticks and I'm unable to swallow, trapping any breath from entering or exiting my lungs. My eyes fill with water. Probably not tears, just water. All I can do is look up into the sky to keep them from falling. You know, macho man appearances and what-not.

"What now?" Jaws asks.

I pause before answering. "Nothing now, Jaws. We've already been through all of this. There's nothing for us to do here anymore. Go back to work for your dad. Learn the family trade. Brew up some kickass liquor, then make a bunch of money. Forget all this club bullshit. It's never done anything good for you. In fact, all it *has* done is get you hooked up on coke, destroy your mandible, give you a cheesy ass nickname, and get your best friend killed. Why do you keep sticking around?"

"It's what Scott wanted," he says quietly, hanging his head and looking at his shoes.

I open my mouth to respond, but my words stick in my throat. I regroup and try again. "I get it. We're all here because of Scott, but you gotta let it go. It's over. There's nothing left of the Kings."

That's not the first time I've said that, but for some reason this time, the words pierce my chest like a knife. It pains me to acknowledge that the Kings of Chaos no longer exist. Sure, that was the goal when I originally returned to my hometown, but I never would've imagined it going down like this.

Jaws doesn't respond. He continues to gaze down at the earth below his feet, then slowly begins to shuffle off back to his car.

I look at Miller. "What now?"

"Well, I haven't brought this up yet, but I have an idea," Miller responds. I'm not sure what he has in mind, but I swear I see a little twinkle in his eye. Unless it's sunlight glinting off of water in his eye too, but I doubt it.

Chapter 24

The drive back to my apartment is mostly quiet, shy of a few sniffles. We pull into the parking lot and I see that my neighbor has guests. She's sitting outside in the grass, playing with her son while an older couple and a middle-aged female stand nearby. I can only assume they're the grandparents that have custody and the case-worker that's assigned to this case.

Miller and I walk by silently. He keeps his eyes down to avoid any awkward encounters, whereas my dumbass seeks out the awkwardness. I meet the eyes of the older couple, who offer slight smiles. I return with a half-grin of my own and a quick nod of my head. It appears they are trying to relay a feeling of gratitude without using words. There's a good chance I'm completely making that up though too. It's my story and that's how I want to see it, so that's what I'm going with.

We reach my front door, and I unlock it to step inside. Before I do, I hear a quick noise that gets my attention.

"Hey."

I turn and look back toward the grassy area where the group is. My neighbor lady looks at me for a second. I immediately recognize that her beady, dead little eyes have some flash of life behind them. Her skin has a more natural color, and her face appears to be more filled out than what I'm used to; all positive signs of somebody in recovery.

"Supervised visitation," she says. "The first step to getting my son back." I smile and nod my head in acknowledgement. "Thank you," she finishes.

"Good luck," I say, sincerely, before breaking eye contact and stepping inside. Holy shit, I was not ready for that. With everything that's happened in the past week, tears pour down my cheeks like somebody turned on a damn faucet. I quickly step through the living room, trying to avoid Miller seeing my face and make a beeline for the bathroom where I sit on the lid of the toilet and have a complete and utter meltdown…silently of course. You know, macho man appearances and what-not.

I turn on the water and let it run to drown out any sissy noises that could escape my body right now. I also use the cold water to rinse my face and try to regain my composure. Luckily, I'm able to get it together in time for Miller to knock on the bathroom door.

"You might want to wrap it up in there," he says through the door. "I think there's something you're gonna want to see out here."

I turn off the water and dry my hands and face as quickly as I can, then step out into the hallway to see what Miller's going on about. He's sitting in the recliner, but his body language appears very attentive. He's on the edge of the chair, leaning forward with his elbows on his knees, his eyes locked on the TV.

"This just in," I hear the reporter from the local network say as I round the corner of the TV stand. "Few details are beginning to trickle in, but we're gathering that the Drug Enforcement Agency has just busted one of the biggest drug rings in their agency's existence. Names have not been released at this time, but we've confirmed that the leader of this drug ring was located just outside of Clarksville, Tennessee, where the bust occurred earlier this morning. It's unclear how many arrests have been made, but our reporter on the scene has been assured by a spokesperson for the DEA that many more are coming. From what we've been able to gather, the distribution ring covers the state of Tennessee and the Commonwealth of Kentucky, with fingers reaching much further than that."

I look at Miller and raise an eyebrow. He smirks back in return. "Crazy timing, huh? Coincidence?" I wonder out loud.

"No chance," he comments. "We just got the Bombers served up to us on the biggest silver platter you could ever imagine."

I sense his excitement, because I'm feeling it too. And just as quickly, my excitement fades to anxiety. My facial expression must relay my change of emotion.

"What?" Miller asks.

"Our timetable just disappeared. We're scheduled to meet with the Bombers tomorrow at noon, but if they realize that Dirty Mike has been taken into federal custody they're going to lash out. They're going to panic, and want to feel like they have control over something. That something is likely gonna be our territory. We need to get ahead of this as much as possible, and handle things on our terms." He nods in agreement. "I need to make a call," I say before stepping out of the living room and into my bedroom.

"Yeah, me too," Miller agrees as I close my bedroom door.

"This all ends tomorrow. You free around noon?" I call out over my shoulder just to be annoying.

First on my to-do list: get ahold of my DEA contact. I scroll through my phone for a second, then hit the green send button as soon as the name appears on my screen. It only rings twice, but I swear they're the two longest rings I've ever heard in my life.

"Yeah?" finally comes the answer from the other end.

"Well hello to you too. Looks like you're staying busy today."

"Will, what do you need? I don't have time for your annoying BS, but I'm assuming you're calling about something that's connected to what I have going on in Tennessee."

"Indeed, Kemosabe." I can hear his eyeroll over the phone from a hundred miles away. "Have any lunch plans tomorrow?" I ask innocently.

"Will, dammit, cut the shit. What are you up to?"

"I have a meeting with the Bombers tomorrow at noon. Think you have any interest in attending?"

Silence hangs on the line for a moment before I get a response. "I'll be there by ten. Meet you at your HQ?"

"Sounds good." I hang up with a grin on my face. I step back out into my living room as Miller is finishing his own call. "This all ends tomorrow," I repeat. He nods.

Chapter 25

Miller and I hardly get any sleep. We're so amped up, we can't help but blab back and forth about what is about to transpire and the endless possibilities about how it could all play out. I tell him it's gonna be anti-climactic – the Bombers show up at noon, the DEA swoops in, arrests are made, and they're all out of town before anybody even knows what happened. He considers it going another way – the Bombers show up knowing about Dirty Mike and have nothing to lose. They outnumber us, back us into our headquarters, then pull their weapons and put an end to us.

"No chance," I dismiss his theory. "That's way too predictable. Besides, that's how things went down last time with the Kings. There's no way this ends the same way. That would just be lazy and unoriginal."

Eventually, we finally succumb to fatigue and end up passing out in the living room for a few hours. The rising sun wakes me with a start. There's fire in my veins, pounding out my pulse like a spark plug firing with every RPM. My heartrate is in overdrive and my thoughts are frantic; What time is it? Is the DEA here yet? Are the Bombers already here? What if Miller's prediction is right? Am I ready for another shootout? Can my body take the punishment from another round?

I'm finally able to get it together when I see that it's only seven in the morning. I hadn't slept through my alarm, I just woke up before it went off. My pulse returns to a normal pace once my brain processes the reality of the situation. I stumble into the bathroom to relieve my bladder. That organ, unlike my heart, is slightly more difficult to relax once it's decided that it's done being helpful.

I decide to jump in the shower while I'm already in the bathroom. The hot water doesn't seem to be able to get hot enough this morning. Regardless, I stand under the water with my back facing the shower head. The warmth that is there trickles down my neck and shoulders, and I can feel the stress and anticipation wash away. The bad news is that it doesn't last. It's only effective until the second I turn the water off, then the tension immediately returns.

I step out of the tub and dry off before brushing my teeth. After that, the time has come to get dressed. I grab my uniform from the closet and give it a quick inspection, ensuring there are no wrinkles and that everything is in the precise place it's supposed to be in. I like to think I have a keen eye for detail, but I really want to make sure everything is perfect for today. You might call it passive-aggressive, me trying to flaunt my position of authority over the Bombers, but I prefer to call it childish.

I return to the living room to lace up my tactical boots, and Miller has already slipped into the bathroom to use up whatever hot water remains. Good luck, sucker.

In no time, it's time to meet my DEA contact at the police station. We drive my pickup and park it front and center along Main Street – directly in front of the building, broadcasting the police presence in my town. I don't want there to be any confusion as to who the Bombers are dealing with when they get here.

I keep my eyes peeled through the window in the front door, to try to spot the federal agent as he arrives. I alternate my focus from Main Street to my watch, then back again. It's not quite ten o'clock, but you could say I'm a little anxious. Without me realizing it, the agent slides into the building through a side door and completely catches me off guard. Miller still shows no expression, like he's incapable of being surprised. That guy just has massive balls of steel. That's all there is to it. And I guarantee they drag the ground as he walks. Just enormous, dangly balls. No way around it.

As I try to shift my focus away from Miller's man-parts, the agent jumps right into his situation report. "Will, I don't know what you have in mind, but here's what I'm thinking. I'm gonna hang back when you meet with these guys. I'll plant some listening devices in here so I can track the conversation. Once I feel like we have the situation under control, then I'll swoop in and make some arrests."

"It's just you?" I ask, incredulous that he wouldn't bring some backup to a meeting of this magnitude. Especially considering the connections to his own bust just yesterday.

"I'm gonna drop back and get out of sight," he says, dismissing my question. "I really don't want to spook these guys before we're ready."

Before he can completely finish his thought, we hear some thunder in the distance. This isn't the kind of thunder that follows a streak of lightening though. This is the kind of thunder that doesn't stop, and only gets louder as it gets closer. The low rumble of motorcycle exhaust pipes. And by my guess, a lot of exhaust pipes.

My eyes widen with a tiny bit of fear. Fear that we aren't ready and this whole freaking thing is about to go sideways before it even starts. The DEA agent bolts for the door, trying to get hidden from sight while he still can.

Miller just stands by the side of his desk showing no emotion at all, except for maybe a grin. A grin? But why? That effing guy.

I peek outside through the window in the front door, waiting to see a whole slew of Bombers ride into town. The scene plays out exactly like I expect, except I don't recognize any of the bikers. I keep watching outside, trying to figure out how to process what's happening. I glance at Miller, and there's no question he's grinning. "What the hell are you grinning about?" I finally ask.

"You got your guys, these are my guys," he responds and steps to the door. I follow him outside and just watch as the scene continues to unfold.

Bike after bike rides through town on Main Street. The line goes on and on as they enter town. They drive past Rusty's Tavern, the Gas N' Go, the boarded-up building that used to be the library, and keep going down to the end of town before making a U-turn and coming back past the police station on the near side of the road. They come to a stop at the entrance of town where the highway turns into Main Street, then walk their bikes back to the curb before dropping their kickstands. They all stay on their bikes until the last one is in position. I can't believe my eyes, but there is a line of bikers down the entire length of Main Street on both sides.

Hundreds of motorcycles line the main artery through my town, and only now is when I finally understand what's going on. As the bikers in front of the police station sit with their backs to the sidewalk, waiting for their comrades to finish filing into town, I finally see the matching patches on the backs of their vests. I hardly want more motorcycle clubs involved in what's about to go down here in the next hour, but I immediately recognize this for what it is.

"Called in some reinforcements of my own," Miller says, watching the massive numbers of motorcycles taking formation throughout our helpless town. The red, white, and blue patches on their backs proudly displayed below their organization's name – Veteran's Guard Motorcycle Riding Organization.

These guys aren't actually a Motorcycle Club in the true sense of a typical club, but they are a national organization that fulfill numerous community service duties throughout their local chapters, primarily pertaining to the assistance of military veterans. These are the guys who escort the families of fallen service members to the airport to receive their loved one's remains. They attend funerals to make sure the surviving family isn't subjected to whack-job protestors. They organize fundraisers for homeless vets, and really just try to look out for those who served and sacrificed for this country.

"This doesn't really seem to be the type of thing these guys get involved with," I comment to Miller.

He responds without breaking focus on the sight in front of him. "I made a call to a buddy I served with from Louisville. I told him a little bit about what we had going on, hoping that maybe I could get a couple helping hands. Once he found out what was happening, and that it was a bunch of former reservists behind it, he was more than happy to make some calls of his own. And now here we are: Operation Shock and Awe in full effect."

"Is shock and awe anything like shake and bake?"

"I'm gonna blame that one on the stress, because that was dumb even for you," he condescends. "There's power in numbers. When the Bombers roll into town, it's not like they're going to see what these patches say. They're just going to ride through that curve onto Main Street and immediately piss themselves when they see all this splayed out in front of them."

Fair point.

"This should be enough to keep them off balance so they reconsider doing anything too stupid," he finishes.

I like it. I like it a lot.

I notice a couple guys approaching us from our left. Miller looks in that direction, then walks to meet them. I assume that's his buddy that he put in his original call to. As they start to chat, I turn and go back inside the station.

I check and double check my sidearm, making sure it's loaded and the safety's off. I pat around my duty belt, triple checking that I have my canister of OC spray, handcuffs, extra magazines for my pistol, then spark test my taser to make sure it's ready to go. All of this is just in case, of course. Ya know, just in case.

Another fifteen minutes pass before I start to pick up the sound of thunder on the horizon again. My head jerks up from the paperwork on my desk at the possibility of it being go-time. I quickly step outside and see Miller has already resumed his position in front of the station, his friends presumably back with their bikes. He turns to look at me. "It's time," he says.

Chapter 26

The Bombers ride into town, and I swear I can see their eyes bulge the second they get a look at the scenery in front of them. Miller's assumption was spot on. They turn on the street that runs right next to the police station, then ride straight up onto the sidewalk in front of me and Miller, cutting us off from the scores of Veteran's Guard.

The Bombers dismount from their bikes and Bruiser begins addressing us immediately, before he even begins his approach. "I'm fed up with this shit right here," he points at me and Miller. "Enough double-dippin' into the outlaw world whenever you want to play biker, then hidin' behind that shield when shit gets real," he accuses. "And there ain't gonna be any sucker punches this time around." He points a finger at Miller, attempting to set the tone of the meeting.

There's a loud chorus of motorcycle engines as the members of the Veteran's Guard fire up their bikes and reposition them, closing off every side street as well as Main Street itself, giving the Bombers nowhere to go. It's so hard to keep the smirk to myself right now.

Miller returns verbal fire to Bruiser. "Don't say any dumb shit and maybe I won't knock your jaw off again."

Threatening people while in uniform usually isn't the best idea, but I have no objections so I let Miller continue. "Take a look around. You're in our town. Surrounded by our brothers, addressing our police force. I don't know where you think you have a leg to stand on here."

"Because I ain't worried about you CHiPS wannabes. If you had anything on us, you woulda already arrested us last week." Enough with the bad Erik Estrada jokes already.

By now, Bruiser and a handful of his guys are standing toe-to-toe with us.

"See, now that right there is the kind of dumb shit I'm referring to. Bring it up again and you'll eat through a straw for the rest of your life," Miller reprimands.

There's no warning. Out of nowhere, Bruiser springs toward Miller. He plants his head into the side of Miller and keeps rushing, trying to get my partner off his feet and onto his back, but Miller's prepared. He spins to his right and flings Bruiser a couple feet away from him. They square off and stare each other down.

"Well that was anti-climactic," I mention. "I expected a lot more than that." I barely finish my sentence before a couple of the guys in front of me swarm and start throwing body blows. I keep my arms tight to my body to try to absorb some of the shots, and take steps back to create space between me and my assailants. Once I've backed up a couple steps I reach out for the closest guy, grabbing his vest and pulling it over his head like I was in a hockey fight. There's a reason those guys use that tactic when they fight, so I decide to give it a shot. It seems pretty straight-forward; you can't really throw a punch if your arms are trapped by your ears. And if you're pulling a shirt over a guy's head, it forces their eyes down to the ground, and you can't hit what you can't see. It really is a brilliant tactic.

The downside of this approach is that it doesn't really work too well when you're getting rat-packed by a bunch of guys at once. It's a numbers game I'm playing here, and I'm losing. The Veteran's Guard is only here as a show of force, not to actually *be* a force…that's not really their thing. Miller and I are on our own. Out of my periphery I see that Bruiser has re-engaged Miller, but that shouldn't be much of a matchup.

As expected, Miller puts Bruiser on the ground and makes his way to my aid. He starts grabbing guys from behind and tossing them aside. Something has snapped inside Miller and he's in a completely different place. I know what's going through my mind as we attempt to fight off this overwhelming ass-whooping, but I can tell Miller's mind is in a completely different mode. I'm analyzing every little movement in slow motion, preparing to react, and planning for my next maneuver, but I can see that his thought process has completely shut off. He's relying solely on training right now. When you have somebody that's highly trained to react in these types of situations without thinking, that can be a very dangerous and scary thing…for the other guys. And the poor bastards don't even know it.

Miller is man-handling these guys like they're tantrum-throwing children. My brain is processing things so quickly I can see movements like they're being telegraphed. The weird thing though, is just because I'm processing things that fast, doesn't mean I can respond that fast. Before I can warn him, I see Bruiser approach Miller from behind. The sun glints off a shiny blade in Bruiser's right hand. I try to yell out to warn Miller, but I fail. The blade slides into Miller's kidney area. He doesn't react as his brain isn't currently accepting stimuli. Bruiser removes the blade and inserts it again before Miller finally recoils from the pain.

Miller instinctively grabs his lower back area and pulls his hand back in front of his face. Bright, crimson red drips from his fingers onto the sidewalk. He drops to a knee and the Bombers jump him immediately, raining down kicks and hammer fists. Bruiser prepares his knife for another shanking when my mind and body finally decide to cooperate.

I pull my sidearm from the holster and level the barrel dead center between Bruiser's eyes. "Don't." Everybody stops dead in their tracks. "I don't know what you asshats thought you were going to accomplish here this afternoon, but this shit ends now. E. Mediately. Make all the cheesy biker cop references you want, but the fact remains. We are officers of the law and you will not come into our town and swing your manhood around like you run things. Maybe you don't watch the news, but your time has come and gone. Mike got arrested yesterday, and today is gonna be your lucky day." I see the Bombers react as I'm laying it all out for them. I can tell they want to run to their bikes and get the hell outta town, but all of their exits have been blocked by hundreds of bikers.

That's when blacked out SUVs enter the scene from every angle, their windshields and grills lighting up with red and blue strobe lights. The Veteran's Guard make way so the tactical vehicles can approach unabated. My DEA friend slides out of the lead SUV. "Will, looks like you guys could use a little backup. I've got plenty of space in these trucks and my guys have extra handcuffs, so I think you're in luck."

I had no idea there was a whole DEA task force in town for this. Damn these guys are good. Although, I might be more appreciative if they would have shown up prior to my partner getting shanked like he was in prison.

Bruiser tenses like he's about to make one more desperate move.

Before his intentions are clear, I swing my pistol toward his head, connecting the unforgiving metal with his temple. He drops to the concrete like a sack of potatoes.

"He's all yours," I say to the DEA agents who are already immersing among the Bombers.

I hear Miranda Rights being recited over the clicking sound of handcuff locks ratcheting around wrists. I kneel down to Miller to make sure he's okay. I throw his arm over my shoulder and help him into the police station while the DEA cleans up the trash outside. "Try not to bleed on my floor," I request. He chuckles lightly, then groans. I'm not sure if the groan is out of pain from the stab wound or my bad joke. It's probably the wound. Gotta be, right?

I have him lay down on his stomach so I can address his injury. I grab the first aid kit from behind my desk and press sterile bandages onto the bloody gash, trying my best to apply pressure to control the bleeding while calling for an ambulance on my radio. "Officer down," are the only words necessary to get an ambulance moving in our direction at warp speed.

Chapter 27

I spend the rest of the morning back in the waiting area of Grayson County Medical Center. Turns out a lacerated kidney is a pretty serious injury. Evidently blood and urine leak out into surrounding tissue and that's not good.

While I'm waiting, I take a walk around the facility. I try to convince myself that I'm wandering aimlessly, but come on let's be serious, I think we all know where I'm headed. I pass the cafeteria and gift shop as I leave the Emergency Department, then walk by the waiting area for the Labor and Delivery wing.

A television grabs my attention as I'm shuffling by. It's turned to the local news, and the story is breaking regarding today's events. The part that I wasn't expecting is how a second bust was made that I had no knowledge of. Evidently, the DEA made a concerted effort to raid the Bombers' clubhouse in Owensboro at the same time of the meeting in Rough River Falls. Talk about prepared and thorough. Those guys never cease to amaze me. I lose interest in the television when the news transitions to a commercial break.

Ultimately, I walk toward the secured Crisis area of the hospital. I pull my credentials from my back pocket and patiently wait to get a nurse's attention as they walk by.

"Excuse me, miss?" I try. "I need to speak with a patient back there." I gesture past the locked doors that are currently keeping me from my destination while flashing my badge. I can tell the nurse isn't quite sure how to respond. Law enforcement officers can typically BS their way through any situation, but HIPAA laws aren't something that medical workers push boundaries on.

"It's urgent," I press. I see her eyes dart around to see if anybody else is nearby. She finally concedes and slaps her key card against the electronic lock on the wall. The doors begin to swing open and I thank her for her assistance.

I approach Kayla's room and my pace slows noticeably. My palms get a little clammy from nervous sweat, and I'm suddenly feeling hesitant. I quietly step into the doorway of her room and watch her for a brief moment before she notices me.

She starts to ask for a cup of ice, sensing that somebody has entered her room, but dismisses that request as soon as she realizes I'm not her nurse. I offer to get a cup for her, but rather than accept my offer, she rolls away from me in her bed. Her long hair is a tangled mess. It doesn't look like she's been out of bed since she was admitted, and for all I know she probably hasn't been.

"I just thought I'd stop by and see how you're doing," I say sheepishly.

"I don't want to see you," she says, ignoring my statement.

I take another step into the room. "Kayla, I'm trying," I plead. "I'm trying to make a difference. I'm trying to fix things and make this place better. I just brought down another MC that was running cocaine like the Kings were. My partner is in surgery trying not to die from wounds he got taking them down today. The source has been detained by the DEA. I'm trying to make sure Scott didn't die for nothing." I stand there for what feels like minutes in silence. I can tell that Kayla has already made up her mind. There's nothing I can say now that'll bring her back to me. My chest hurts, just wanting her to acknowledge me. "I'm sorry," I say quietly before turning to leave the room, finally admitting to myself and conceding to the fact that she's gone. I get back to the doorway when she finally speaks to me, stopping me dead in my tracks.

"Will. The doctors have discovered something since I've been in here. They found something in my blood they weren't expecting." I stand with my back to her, waiting to see where this is going. "Will...I'm pregnant."

About the author

Charles Kelley grew up in the foothills of southern Indiana. He fled the farm lands upon graduation from high school to attend Ball State University. After receiving a B.S. in Criminal Justice/Criminology, he started his career working with various criminal justice agencies. His writing career started very modestly with a personal blog, which developed his love of creative writing, leading to his webpage of short stories. Naturally, the next step was developing bigger ideas and longer stories, AKA novels, so here we are.

He currently resides in Indianapolis, Indiana and is trying his best to raise a family, further his career, and explore his interest in writing. Any other "free time" is occupied by watching sports, riding his motorcycle, playing guitar, and traveling.

Keep up to date with news on upcoming projects by following Charles on social media:
www.facebook.com/ckwriting
www.instagram.com/ckfiction
www.twitter.com/ckfiction

You can also check out his humble beginnings by reading some of his short stories at www.ckfiction.com.

CPSIA information can be obtained
at www.ICGtesting.com
Printed in the USA
FSHW04n0851300318
46267FS